"You've heard the story, I know you have."

Nicholas concluded his speech. "And so, Miss-Tish-Holmsworth-of-the-Laketown-Herald, that is why I must never see you again."

Desperately Tish cast about in her mind for some way to convince Nicholas he was on the wrong track. "That was a nice speech," she said finally, trying to look as directly at Nicholas as he had at her. "You think you are being noble, but I think you're being arrogant. What makes you think you can decide what I'm supposed to think and what I'm supposed to want?"

"Stop it, Tish!" Nicholas bent so close that his breath was warm upon her lips as he spoke. "Believe me, I understand what must be, far better than you can. I wasn't being noble. Look at this face. Think about what you know about me. Can you honestly say you would ever consider marrying me?"

Katherine Arthur is full of life. She describes herself as a writer, research associate (she works with her husband, a research professor in experimental psychology), farmer, housewife, proud mother of five and a grandmother to boot. The family is defintely full of overachievers. But what she finds most interesting is the diversity of occupations the children have chosen—sports medicine, computers, finance and neuroscience (pioneering brain tissue transplants), to name a few. Why, the possibilities for story ideas are practically limitless.

Books by Katherine Arthur

HARLEQUIN ROMANCE

Don't miss any of our special offers. Write to us at the following address for information on our newest releases.

Harlequin Reader Service
901 Fuhrmann Blvd., P.O. Box 1397, Buffalo, NY 14240
Canadian address: P.O. Box 603,
Fort Erie, Ont. L2A 5X3

Through Eyes of Love

Katherine Arthur

Harlequin Books

TORONTO • NEW YORK • LONDON
AMSTERDAM • PARIS • SYDNEY • HAMBURG

Original hardcover edition published in 1988
by Mills & Boon Limited

ISBN 0-373-02991-8

Harlequin Romance first edition July 1989

Through Eyes of Love
Condemned for deeds and scars
            for years gone by,
He left the world alone,
            as it left him.
Her heart erased the flaws
            that others saw.
Through eyes of love,
            she saw a perfect man.
                        Barbara Eriksen

CHAPTER ONE

THE bearded man leaned forward on his cane and peered short-sightedly at Tish's conference badge. 'Letitia Holmsworth, *Laketown Herald*, Laketown, New York,' he read. He raised his head and looked into Tish's eyes with an almost frightening intensity. 'I knew a man from Laketown, New York once. In Vietnam. His name was Nicholas Morgan. He was the bravest man I ever knew. He gave his life for me.'

Tish stared at the man. 'Nicholas Morgan?' she said. 'But . . .'

'Hey, Charlie, old buddy, the ladies are waiting.' A chunky, balding man came up and clapped an arm around the bearded stranger's shoulders. 'Let's get the show on the road,' he said jovially.

The bearded man nodded and turned away.

'But Nicholas Morgan . . . isn't dead,' Tish said softly. In the crowd, the man did not hear. A familiar, high-pitched voice distracted her. She turned to look. 'Nancy!' she cried.

'Tish! Tish Holmsworth!' The tiny blonde woman waved, then pushed her way through the crowd to Tish's side and flung her arms around her.

'Nancy Smith!' Tish squealed, hugging the woman back. 'Of all people to run into! What on earth are you doing here? You aren't actually in the newspaper business now too, are you?'

'I sure am. I married Fred Atkins, remember him? He was the boy I went with when we were seniors back at good old Cornell. Fred got transferred to Iowa, and when I found out there wasn't any newspaper in our little town, I started one. I *am* the *MacKenzie Iowa Republican*.'

'Fantastic!' Tish replied. 'But you are the world's worst letter-writer. Tell me all about everything.'

She and Nancy had talked for ages, Tish remembered. They had arranged to share a hotel room at the convention of small-town newspaper editors in Chicago, and had chattered on until the wee hours every night about their lives since their college days. The convention had lasted for three days, but Tish had not seen the bearded man again. The encounter had been forgotten. Until now, at a rock concert in Lakefront Park in Laketown, New York, the following September.

The huge amplifiers blared a final crescendo, the strobe lights flashed a dizzying climax of colours, and Mike O'Hara, known to his screaming fans as The Monster, struck a dramatic pose, then bent double. Whether it was a bow or some sort of seizure, Tish was not sure. She had scarcely heard his final song, her attention had been so divided between that and the sight of Nicholas Morgan, standing not more than ten feet away. He almost never appeared in public, yet there he stood, perfectly still, towering about the writhing mob of teenagers, his hair gleaming like burnished copper in the strobe lights, his face stern and impassive. The ugly Y-shaped scar which encompassed his right cheek and ended below his set, angular jaw seemed to glow grotesquely in the skittering lights.

'I wonder what he's doing here?' Mavis Greer said, up close to Tish's ear.

'I wonder too,' Tish replied.

Mavis shrugged. 'Well, I've got to go. I'll see you at the party.'

Tish nodded vaguely, her mind still on Nicholas Morgan and the memory of her encounter in Chicago. It was probably not surprising that the bearded man had thought Nicholas was dead. He had been badly wounded, she knew, in the hospital for over a year. There was another, smaller scar on his other cheek. He wore the scars defiantly, like an emblem of his travail, although there was no doubt he could have afforded the most skilful plastic surgeons to work their magic. Nicholas Morgan was now, since his father's death, the owner of the Morgan Wineries, the finest in New York, famous throughout the world for their light, delicate champagnes. He could, if he chose, go anywhere, do anything. Instead, he kept to himself at Castlemont, the huge, castle-like mansion on the hill above his ancestral vineyards. From there he conducted the business of the wineries. His only excursions into the outside world were either related to that business, or to show the magnificent horses which he raised. And yet . . . here he was, at a rock concert. It was the last place that Tish would have expected to see him, and the first time in many years that she had seen him this close. It was no wonder, she thought, that he tended to stay out of sight. But why had he come here? He was the same age as Hal Greer, Mavis's brother, and Mike O'Hara, some ten years older than Tish. The three men had been good friends, in their carefree high-school days. Tish had seen Nicholas Morgan often then, but had paid little heed. She had only shadowy memories of him and the crowd of older boys, who had treated her and Mavis, playing with their dolls on the Greer's big front porch, as little more than an annoyance. In the intervening years, she had seen him

only once or twice from a distance, and had not spoken
to him at all. And, as far as she knew, he had had no
more contact with his former high-school friends than
with anyone else.

The crowd was jostling Tish towards the stage.

'Wasn't he fantastic?' said a teenage girl, turning a
pair of wide blue eyes, made up with sparkling gold and
purple shadow, towards Tish.

'Oh, absolutely,' Tish replied, reminded that she was
here to do a story on Mike O'Hara, the home-town boy
who had become the idol of millions. She reached up
and gingerly touched the green, spiky-looking wig that
she had worn on the insistence of Mavis's younger sister,
Mona.

'The kids won't talk to you if you look like an old
person,' Mona had warned her, and so Tish had bor-
rowed some outlandish clothes and bought a cheap
blonde wig and dyed it bluish green. The colour, she
observed, might look fine for her eyes, but was perfectly
dreadful for hair. The wig, along with some suitably
weird make-up, had worked, managing to turn an ancient
twenty-seven-year-old into a teenager for the night. She
had had plenty of good interviews, and would be able
to satisfy the Laketown natives that their former high-
school bad boy was, indeed, adored by his fans, who
had come from as far away as Albany to hear him play
at Lakefront Park.

As the crowd pushed and shoved, hoping for another
glimpse of their hero, Tish saw that Nicholas Morgan,
too, was being carried along in the same direction. He
was now only a few feet in front of her. Should she talk
to him? That was, she knew, the only way she was going
to find out why he had come. He certainly wouldn't call
up the newspaper and tell her. The only information she

ever got about his movements was through a secretary, who occasionally gave out a Press release about the wineries, or from a horse show chairman, who would reveal that Nicholas Morgan's horses had won yet another prize. Would he talk to her? She doubted he would recognise her. He might not even remember her. Well, there was only one way to find out.

Tish stuck her elbows out and plunged ahead, prying between bodies until she had only one more between her and her quarry. She stopped, her heart beating faster. Nicholas Morgan had paused at the edge of the stage. He was staring pensively across the now darkened footlights, as if he were seeing far beyond the scurrying technicians, the tangle of instruments and backdrops that remained.

'Here goes nothing,' Tish muttered to herself, taking a deep breath. She walked over to Nicholas Morgan. 'Mr Morgan?' she said, then almost recoiled as he turned his head and looked directly down at her. The ugly scar was partially hidden in the shadows now, but his eyes were the lightest, clearest blue she had ever seen, and they were hauntingly, icily cold. It was a cold that, Tish thought, looked as lonely as a vast expanse of Arctic ice.

'Yes?' he replied, in a deep, husky voice.

'I—I'm Tish Holmsworth, from the *Laketown Herald*,' she said fumbling in her jacket pocket and producing her Press identification. 'I don't know if you remember...'

Nicholas Morgan glanced at the card and then raised one jagged eyebrow, looking pointedly at Tish's green hair.

'Oh.' Tish laughed nervously and snatched the wig from her head, then ran her fingers through her short brown curls. 'My disguise, so I could talk to the fans,' she explained. When Nicholas said nothing, only raised the other eyebrow to join the first, she went on, 'I was surprised to see you here. I wondered if you'd tell me how you happened to come. Is it because you and Mike used to be friends, or because you like rock music?'

The unflickering cold stare returned to meet Tish's eyes. After what seemed to Tish like several minutes, Nicholas shook his head very slightly.

'Neither,' he said. 'I would appreciate it if you wouldn't mention that I was here.'

For a moment Tish felt angry. It was a free country, and she could mention that Nicholas Morgan was at the rock concert if she darn well pleased. She frowned, staring levelly back into those icy blue eyes. It was an almost dizzying experience, like looking deep into a bottomless lake, of the clearest water.

'All right,' she agreed suddenly, not sure exactly why she did so.

'Thank you.' There was a brief flicker of warmth in the icy blue. 'If you'll excuse me, I must go now. Good evening, Miss Holmsworth.'

'Good...evening,' Tish said, watching as Nicholas Morgan pushed past a few remaining fans, thrust his hands deep into his pockets and, head down, walked off into the darkness. How odd, she thought, that a man so courageous should behave as if he were some sort of pariah.

The vision of Nicholas Morgan making his lonely exit into the night still on her mind, Tish made her way to the back of the stage and showed her Press pass to one of Mike O'Hara's burly guards.

'Mike's already gone to some party,' the guard said.

'I know,' Tish replied. 'At Hal Greer's. I'm going there myself in a few minutes. I'd just like to have a look around, if you don't mind. Get a little extra colour for my article.'

'Go ahead,' said the guard. 'Be my guest.'

Tish wandered about through the maze of cords, glittering instruments and busy technicians, trying to make some mental notes, but with her mind only partially on her task. Seeing and actually talking to Nicholas Morgan had left her feeling unaccountably shaken and confused, as if, deep inside, she felt that something far more important than Mike O'Hara's triumphant return to Laketown had happened.

But, she told herself as she found her car in the maelstrom of vehicles and headed for the party, that was ridiculous. It was not exactly earth-shattering news that Nicholas Morgan had finally decided to leave his lair and find out what the real world was doing. The people of Laketown and the neighbouring villages would be interested, of course, but there had doubtless been enough other natives who had seen Nicholas for the word to spread through the grapevine. She did not have to print it in the *Laketown Herald*.

'Good lord, I thought you'd got lost,' Mavis greeted Tish when at last she arrived at the Greers' big wooden house perched on a hillside above Laketown College.

'I stopped to talk to some people,' Tish said. 'Where's the hero of the night? I haven't even said hello to him yet.'

'Right this way,' Mavis said, taking Tish's arm and leading her through the mob of old friends who had come to see their former schoolmate. 'He's holding court by the bar with all of his old buddies.'

'My God, you've grown up to be a gorgeous lady,' Mike greeted Tish with effusive warmth. 'If you'd been my age, I'd never have left home. You got a steady boyfriend, or do I still have a chance?'

'She's got one of the young deans at the college dancing to her tune,' Hal Greer put in. 'Where is old Larry tonight? Too good for us simple folk?'

'He's not a rock fan,' Tish replied, 'and besides, he thought he'd feel a bit of an outsider, with everyone here having known each other for so long.' Having to make excuses for Larry Johnson made her feel uncomfortable. She had tried to persuade him to come, but he had been adamant, even though she had explained several times that she would feel as much an outsider as he. She and Mavis, her long-time friend, were going to be the only ones from their generation at the party.

'Well, we sure have known each other for ever, haven't we, old pal?' Mike said, putting an arm around Hal's shoulders.

'Almost from the day we were born,' Hal agreed. 'Let's drink a toast to old friendships, the older the better. Come on, everybody, join in.'

Glasses were raised all around, and soon stories were flying back and forth of shared remembrances. Some were stories of pranks the men had played on each other, some were more serious. There had been the usual ration of tragedies, and several of the men had been to war. Tish listened silently, mentally trying to make herself feel part of their lives, so that the article she would write would have the proper perspective.

'All in all, I'd say we were a pretty lucky group,' Hal said into a moment of silence.

'Yeah, pretty lucky,' Mike agreed, although his expression was grim, and Tish guessed that he was thinking of his brother, Kevin, who had not returned from Vietnam.

'You'll never guess who I saw at the concert,' said a tall, thin man, whom Tish did not remember. 'Nicholas Morgan.'

'No kidding?' said someone.

'I wonder why?' said another.

But Tish did not look at them. She was watching Mike O'Hara, who at first turned pale, and then gradually became beet-red with fury.

'That lousy so and so,' he snarled, following his first statement with a string of unflattering expletives.

A sudden silence fell on the group around the bar, all eyes now on Mike O'Hara.

'Sorry about the swearing, ladies,' he said, turning his black frown on Tish and Mavis, 'but there's nothing else strong enough to describe the yellow-bellied coward that killed my brother. And I used to think he was my best friend.' He spat out the last words contemptuously.

'Not now, Mike,' Hal said into the shocked silence. 'This is no time to dredge up old wounds. Besides, he didn't actually kill Kevin.'

'He might as well have,' Mike replied, ignoring Hal's plea, his countenance still furious. 'He led his platoon into a trap that any fool could have seen, got them all wiped out except him and me. And all because he was too damned scared to go the way he was supposed to go. That's the way it was. There's no other way to tell it. It's a good thing I didn't see him tonight, or I might have come down from the stage and...'

'That's enough, Mike,' Hal said warningly.

There was a general low murmur of conversation. Then someone tactfully interceded, 'Hey, Mike, re-

member the time we stole old Nick's favourite horse and
got him hitched up to the milk wagon?'

As if suddenly aware of the damper he was putting
on the party, Mike shook off his gloomy look and
grinned. 'Yeah,' he said, 'and remember when we got
you in trouble with your dad by stealing his car keys and
hiding his new Cadillac in Hal's garage? We really had
him convinced you'd driven it to Buffalo to see your
girlfriend.'

The air of conviviality returned, but Tish could not
keep her mind on the conversation. Her mind was filled
with images of the strange, scarred man, and the two
completely opposite views she had heard of his character. She finally got a few minutes alone with Mike
O'Hara to ask him about his successful career, then ex-
cused herself from the party, pleading that she had a
newspaper to get out and a story to write.

It was well after midnight when Tish left her small
office at the *Laketown Herald*. The story about Mike
O'Hara had flowed rather easily through the keys of her
ancient typewriter, as if it were so trivial that it required
only a small part of her skill. All the while, in the back
of her mind, was lodged the persistent feeling that there
was another story that mattered a great deal more. The
story of Nicholas Morgan.

Funny, she mused as she drove home through the de-
serted streets of the small town, how little she had
thought about Nicholas Morgan in recent years. When
she had thought of him at all, it had been a stereotyped
view of a rich, embittered man, whose past experiences
had somehow twisted his mind so that he had become
a recluse. She had absorbed the commonly expressed
opinion that, if he were really right in the head, he would
have something done about those dreadful scars. People

would usually remark that it was really very sad. He had been such a handsome boy, always good-natured and full of fun, never acting stand-offish or uppity, in spite of his family's wealth. This observation was usually followed by condemnation of him for letting his experiences in the war destroy all that. After all, people would say, others had it just as bad and they didn't let it get them down. And they didn't have all of Nicholas Morgan's money, either!

Obviously, Tish thought now, Mike O'Hara's story of Nicholas Morgan's cowardice had not been widely known, or she would have heard it before. Judging from Hal's anxious warning and from the hush that had fallen at the party at Mike's outburst, it had been a secret between his former close friends. Why let it out now? Nicholas Morgan must know it only too well. Now, if she knew local gossip, the story would quickly make the rounds, adding to the burden of scorn that the reclusive man bore. Was there nothing that he could, or would, say on his own behalf?

'I've got to talk to Nicholas Morgan,' Tish muttered to herself as she parked her car in the narrow, tree-shaded driveway beside the small brick bungalow on the town side of the college campus. 'I wish Dad were here.'

The house where Tish lived was really her father's house, but he was seldom home. A colonel in the regular army, Neil Holmsworth had retired when Tish was still a baby to the small town in the Finger Lakes region of New York state where he had grown up. It was he who had brought the floundering *Laketown Herald* back to life, but, when his wife died when Tish was just out of college, he turned the paper over to Tish. He began travelling, pursuing a lifelong interest in early American Indian cultures, and receiving scholarly acclaim for his writings on the topic. A quiet, stern man himself, who preferred his books and research to the company of others, he might have some ideas on how she could approach the man that Nicholas Morgan had become. She opened the side door, starting as a huge spotted cat came tearing up the short flight of stairs to the door and raced into the kitchen ahead of her.

'Maybe you could tell me, Rocky,' Tish said to the cat, who had assumed his usual nonchalant three-legged sitting position, a crippled forepaw held up before him as if he were ready to do battle. 'You've never let your battle scars get you down, have you? But then...' she picked the cat up and hugged him '... you know that I love you, don't you?' Did Nicholas Morgan know, she wondered, that somewhere there was a man who thought he was the bravest man he'd ever known? Or did he know only the story that his old friend Mike O'Hara had told tonight? Or was there something else that made him bitter? He was so alone. No family any more to love him. Never any rumours of romance. Tish felt her eyes grow misty. No one should have to face life so completely alone. Even when things were going well, it wasn't easy.

Feeling a sudden sympathetic twinge of loneliness, Tish looked at her watch. It was still before midnight in Phoenix, Arizona, where her father was currently staying, and it had been more than a month since she had talked to him. She picked up her phone and punched out his number.

'Hi, Dad,' she said when he answered. 'How's everything with you?' They exchanged pertinent details of their lives easily for several minutes until her father touched on the topic Tish had been hoping he would avoid.

'How are you and Larry getting along?' he asked.

'Oh, just fine,' she answered warily.

'Set a wedding date yet?' her father persisted.

'Don't push Larry at me, Dad,' Tish warned. 'I'm not at all sure that he's the man for me.'

'You could do a lot worse.'

'Mmm-hmm,' Tish said non-committally. She quickly changed the subject. 'Say, Dad, you remember Nicholas Morgan, don't you? I saw him at Mike O'Hara's big triumphal return concert tonight... Yes, he's still a recluse, but I'd like to talk to him.' She went on to explain that her curiosity had been aroused, but omitted any reference to the two opposing views of his character that she had heard. 'I was wondering,' she concluded, 'if you'd have any idea how I might approach him.'

'Hmm,' Neil Holmsworth said thoughtfully, and Tish could picture him frowning and taking an extra puff on his pipe. 'I'm not sure you should approach him, Tish,' he said finally. 'I'm not altogether comfortable about the character of a man who would withdraw from society as he has.'

'It's his character I'm interested in,' Tish said. 'I'm not a child, you know. I'd like to find out what he's really like, instead of accepting second-hand gossip as the truth.'

Her father cleared his throat. 'Well,' he said, in his best reluctant parent's voice, 'you know I'm not one for invading a person's privacy, and I'm sure the last thing the man wants is pity. You'd have to come up with something he'd be interested in, but I don't know what that might be. His horses? The winery? Whatever you do, be cautious.'

'Yes, Dad,' Tish said patiently. 'And thanks for the suggestions.' But after the conversation was over she rejected both topics. Both were too big for a first attempt at talking to Nicholas Morgan. She needed something smaller, something to break the ice. What could it be? What else might interest the man enough so that he would be willing to talk to her?

'I just don't know what to do,' Tish said the next morning, staring out through the windows of the *Laketown Herald* office at the passing traffic.

'I thought we were going out to lunch,' Larry Johnson said, a teasing grin lighting his handsome face. 'Is that suddenly a big problem for you?'

'Oh, for heaven's sake, no,' Tish replied, making a face at him. She took her purse from her desk drawer and stood up. 'It's just that I've had six calls this morning from people who saw Nicholas Morgan at the concert last night. They all want to know if I'm going to print something about it, like "What was the great Nicholas Morgan doing at a rock concert?" or "Has Nicholas Morgan finally decided to come down from his mountain?"'

'Well, are you?' Larry asked. 'It sounds newsworthy to me.'

'No, I'm not!' Tish replied, suddenly positive that she would keep her promise to Nicholas Morgan. 'It sounds too much like some kind of cheap tabloid article. You know, the "Two-Headed Lady Learns to sing a Duet" kind of trash. If the man wants to attend a concert, that's his business.'

Larry frowned. 'Why protect him? From what I've heard, the man's a weird character, hiding up there in that mansion of his with some kind of terrible scars. No wonder the people are curious about him. Don't you think they deserve whatever titbits you can find?'

'Titbits?' Tish looked at Larry's smooth, unmarred face, finding its perfection suddenly more annoying than attractive. He looked so young, so perfect, even though he was only a year younger than Nicholas Morgan. Probably the most traumatic thing that had ever happened to him when he was younger was finding out that he couldn't borrow his father's car for a date. 'Somehow,' she said coldly, 'I don't think I should print *titbits* about someone who's been through what Mr Morgan has been through.'

'All right, all right!' Larry put up his hands as if to protect himself. 'But I still think ...' He stopped, as Tish glared at him.

'I would like to talk to the man,' she said. 'If I could only think of some really good reason to do so, I would, but so far I can't.'

'So far?' Larry raised his eyebrows. 'I didn't know that was on your agenda. I'm not sure I like the idea of your bearding that particular lion in his den.'

'I doubt you need to worry about it,' Tish replied. She let Larry help her into her chair at the small restaurant, just across Laketown's main street from the newspaper office. The waitress who brought their menus greeted them with a friendly smile and called them by name, and several of the other patrons welcomed them with hellos. Tish smiled back and responded, but inside she felt cross and uncomfortable. Everything was so warm, so friendly, so secure and familiar. Why should she feel this way? She scowled at the menu, chewing her lip.

'Are you in a foul mood today, or am I missing something?' Larry said softly.

Tish looked up quickly and smiled, feeling guilty. 'It's nothing,' she said. 'I'm just tired. It was after midnight when I got through with my story about Mike O'Hara.

I think I need more than six hours' sleep.' There was no point in revealing to Larry that of the six hours she had spent in bed, a good half had been used in brooding about Nicholas Morgan, the strange dichotomy of viewpoints she had heard, and a fruitless search for something he might be willing to talk to her about. Finding that thoughts about another man, especially that 'weird character', had kept her awake, would doubtless sour his disposition too.

For the rest of the meal, and for days afterwards, Tish tried valiantly to put thoughts of Nicholas Morgan from her mind. There was, after all, nothing she could do. If the man wanted to be alone, it was his prerogative. She couldn't very well go knocking on his door and then plunge into the topic that so concerned her. It would certainly appear that she was motivated by pity. Well, was she? She wasn't sure, but the more she thought about it, the more she thought not. She wanted to know the man, to find out what made him tick. Only then would she really know how, and even if, she should tell him about the man in Chicago. Maybe he already knew. Perhaps, if she were to tell him, he would simply say, 'So what?' and throw her out on her ear. If only she could find some way to approach him...

CHAPTER TWO

IT WAS early October when a way suddenly presented itself. Tish had just picked up a stack of posters advertising the race for wheelchair athletes that the *Laketown Herald* was sponsoring. The *Herald* was contributing trophies for the winners, but each participant was to find a sponsor, who would pay a certain amount for each half-mile the participant covered. The money was to be donated to purchase equipment for the local rehabilitation centre.

'I wonder,' Tish mused aloud as she studied the poster, 'if I could convince Nicholas Morgan to sponsor someone?' She had already sent letters to all of the business people in the area, but had found that a personal visit was frequently necessary to get a commitment. Morgan Wineries was one of the businesses which had not, as yet, replied. Could she, as Larry put it, beard that particular lion in his den? If he had any sympathy in his heart for someone who had also suffered a disabling misfortune, it might work.

She went back into the newspaper office and plopped the pile of posters on her desk. 'Jeff,' she called to the high-school boy who helped her out after school, 'can you take these posters around now?'

'Sure thing, Miss Holmsworth,' he said. 'You want me to put some up at the school, too?'

'Of course. There are several participants from there. Tell me, do you know if they all have sponsors yet?'

'I don't know. I don't think Peggy Willson has any. She was going to ask some people, but she's so shy now I doubt if she has.'

'Peggy Willson. She's the pretty little blonde girl who was injured in that terrible car accident two years ago, isn't she? How is she getting along?'

Jeff shook his tousled head. 'She gets around OK, but she still doesn't smile very much. I guess when you used to be a cheerleader, sitting in a wheelchair isn't much fun.'

'I'm sure it isn't.' Tish bit her lip thoughtfully. 'I think I'll go and see her this evening. I just may have a idea for a sponsor for her.'

'I think you're off your rocker,' Larry said, when Tish told him over the phone of her plan. 'You'll never even get to see the man. Mind if I come along when you talk to Peggy? I don't want you giving the girl any false hopes.'

'All right, come along,' Tish said with a sigh.

'How about dinner with me first, then?' Larry asked.

'No, not tonight,' Tish replied. 'I've got to clean up some leftovers. Pick me up at seven, OK?'

'All right,' Larry agreed, but Tish could tell he was peeved. She sighed again. Larry prided himself on being practical, but it usually impressed her as being more negative than useful. Maybe, if he were more like she was, inclined to rush ahead when her emotions were aroused, she might have said yes by now to his frequent proposals of marriage. As it was, she simply could not get swept away by being reminded what a solid, stable job Larry had, and what good prospects for advancement.

Promptly at seven, Larry arrived and together they went to the Willsons' home. In spite of Larry's warnings,

Tish had little trouble convincing Peggy that it was worth a try to get the sponsorship of Nicholas Morgan, especially since getting a man of his wealth interested in the rehabilitation centre could be a worthwhile side benefit. 'If he won't do it, we'll just try someone easier next,' she promised the girl.

'I still don't think you two should go up to the mansion alone,' Larry grumbled. 'At least let me drive you there.'

'Definitely not,' Tish replied. 'We'd never get past old Titus at the gate house with you along.'

'What makes you think you can without me?' Larry demanded.

'He's an old friend of my father's,' Tish replied.

'And I know him pretty well, too,' Peggy volunteered. 'He and his wife come to our house for dinner sometimes.'

'Terrific! There, you see?' Tish said triumphantly, as Larry still frowned. 'We're a cinch to at least get on to the grounds. Tomorrow's Saturday. Shall we try it right after lunch?'

'It's OK with me,' Peggy agreed.

Tish felt far less confident the next day, as she and Peggy followed the winding road that led into a valley at the end of the lake, and then up into the hills where the Morgan vineyards thrived. There was a knot in her stomach, and she found it difficult to keep up a light-hearted conversation with Peggy.

'Are you nervous?' Peggy finally asked, after a long silence.

'I'm afraid so,' Tish confessed. 'I just hope I actually get to see Mr Morgan and don't have to leave our letter for him.' She had had Peggy write a letter explaining her need of a sponsor, and had included an instant photo that Tish had taken of the pretty young girl just before they left.

'There's the place,' Peggy said, indicating a large iron sign, arching between two huge brick pillars. 'Castlemont. I used to ride bikes up here sometimes and try to peep in and see the house. Titus wouldn't let me go in, though.'

'Let's hope we can talk him into it today,' Tish said, crossing her fingers. She stopped her car in front of the iron gates and waited for the elderly man to appear. 'Hello, Titus,' she said through her opened window. 'We need to see the lord and master.' She got out of her car and drew him aside to explain their quest. The old man appeared reluctant at first, but when Tish told him that Peggy's schoolmate, Jeff, said she hardly ever smiled any more and that some encouragement was definitely needed, his kindly old eyes filled with tears. 'Go ahead,' he said gruffly. 'I just hope it doesn't cost me my job.'

'If it does, I'll make it front-page news,' Tish promised him, 'and I won't hesitate to tell Mr Morgan that, either.'

The road led upward through a thick stand of pines, obviously planted in neat rows by some earlier Morgan. Suddenly the pines ended, and before them was a huge, meticulously groomed lawn, surrounding the biggest, most elaborate, turret-bedecked castle that Tish had ever seen, its actual presence far more impressive than the photographs she had seen.

'Wow,' Peggy said in awed tones. 'It looks like something straight from Transylvania.'

'It certainly does,' Tish agreed, feeling another chill of nervousness add itself to her tension. She gave Peggy a quick smile. 'But it's just a big, old, American imitation. Well, here I go. If I have any luck, I'll have Mr Morgan come out to meet you.'

Feeling rather shaky, Tish mounted the imposing set of steps to a huge oak door. It took her a moment to discover the doorbell, the frame was so massive. She took a deep breath, then gave the button a firm push. In only seconds, the door was opened by a formally attired manservant, so elderly and frail-looking that it seemed a strong wind might whisk him away.

'Yes?' he said, giving Tish, in her dark, tailored suit, a cold appraisal.

'I would like to see Mr Morgan,' she said. 'Tell him that Miss Holmsworth is here, please.'

'Mr Morgan does not see anyone,' the servant replied.

Tish moved into the opened doorway. 'Tell him I'm here, anyway,' she said.

The servant looked at Tish's determined face for a moment, then bowed his head very slightly. 'Very well,' he said. 'Step inside.'

Her hands clenched together in nervousness, Tish stood still in the cavernous foyer, her heart beating rapidly. So far, so good. At least she was getting a good, long look at this place, and it was like something from a Hollywood movie set for an especially gory murder mystery. The floor was a parqueted pattern of various colours of marble, from black to deep blood red to white. Towards the back, an immense staircase curved upwards, an armoured figure, clutching a double-bitted axe, guarding the bottom. All about were various massive pieces of furniture, doubtless priceless antiques. The servant had drifted silently through a door which opened into an adjoining room. Tish could barely hear low sounds of conversation. Then she could clearly hear something much louder, obviously intended for her ears, in Nicholas Morgan's distinctive, deep voice.

'Show Miss Holmsworth out. I will not see her. And have Titus come up here immediately.'

For a moment, Tish felt a hurt so deep that tears sprang to her eyes. Nicholas Morgan would not see her. Why? What had she done to make him dislike her? Then she remembered her mission, and anger took over. What on earth was wrong with that man? Couldn't he at least speak to her civilly, and in person? She was darned if she would put up with this kind of treatment from anyone! Before the hapless servant could convey any message, she pulled the letter Peggy had prepared from her bag and thrust it toward him, scowling darkly.

'Give this to Mr Morgan,' she said, so loudly, in her effort to be certain that Nicholas Morgan could hear her, that the servant flinched visibly. 'And tell him that if he doesn't respond to it, he's the most penurious, penny-pinching skinflint alive, and I'll label him that on the front page of the *Herald*! And you can tell him, too,' she added to the servant, who was staring at her as if he could believe neither his eyes nor his ears, 'that if he gives Titus any trouble, that will be on the front page, too.'

The servant took the letter, looking first at it, and then at Tish's angry face.

'Well, go on, take it to him now,' she yelled even louder, pointing toward the door from whence Nicholas Morgan's voice had come. 'I'm not leaving until I'm sure you have. Mr Morgan can read, can't he?'

'Oh, yes, miss,' the servant said, turning and almost scurrying in the direction Tish was pointing.

As soon as the servant opened that door, Tish jerked open the huge front door and went outside, slamming the door behind her. She ran down the stairs, got quickly into her car, and wheeled around with a screech of the tyres.

'What happened?' Peggy asked, her own voice trembling at the sight of Tish, with tears streaming down her cheeks.

'The man's impossible. I didn't even get to see him,' Tish answered, dashing the tears from her cheeks impatiently. She tried to smile. 'Maybe the letter will still do some good. I did make sure he got it.'

'Don't feel so bad,' Peggy said comfortingly. 'You said no one ever gets to see Mr Morgan.'

'B-but...' Tish shook her head. It didn't make much sense, the miserable ache that now had invaded her heart. Why had she wanted to see Nicholas Morgan so desperately? He obviously didn't want to see her, ever! She stopped at the gate and gave Titus the bad news.

'He hasn't called me up to the house yet,' Titus said, shrugging philosophically. 'I'll let you know if he does, Letitia.'

'You do that,' Tish replied, 'because I darn well meant exactly what I said.' She managed to calm her temper while she took Peggy home, but then decided to go and sit on one of the benches along the lakefront for a while. If she went to either the newspaper office or her house, Larry would quickly track her down, and she did not feel like facing his 'I told you so' right away. In fact, she thought crossly, she didn't feel like seeing him at all.

By Monday morning, Tish was in no better humour. The day before, Larry had tried to be understanding of her reaction to Nicholas Morgan's rejection, but he had inadvertently touched on the sore spot that had driven Tish to want to see him.

'I know it wasn't just the money. You were trying to do something kind for two people who you think need some help,' he said. 'It's not your fault that one of them isn't willing to be helped. Maybe he knows deep down that he doesn't deserve it.'

'Maybe he just thinks he doesn't,' Tish replied stubbornly.

'Tish,' Larry said patiently, 'I've talked to some of the people who were at the party with Mike O'Hara, and I've heard about what Morgan did in Vietnam. Maybe the man should try to get over his guilt by now, but that's his decision to make, if he can.'

'What do you mean, if he can?' Tish demanded.

Larry shrugged. 'Maybe the guilt is so strong that he can't really think straight about it. Such things happen.'

Tish frowned. If Larry was right, it was more important than ever that she talk to Nicholas Morgan. She thought momentarily of telling Larry about her encounter with the bearded man in Chicago, but decided against it. He would probably come up with a hundred practical reasons why she might question the man's statement, since he apparently didn't know Nicholas Morgan well enough to know that he had survived. He might even think she had made the whole thing up, as negative as he had been about her desire to talk to Nicholas Morgan. She didn't like that attitude of his at all. 'I still want to talk to him,' she said defiantly. 'I *am* going to talk to him!' But how that was going to come about, except possibly through some other closed door, she had no idea.

She was still brooding about it, between efforts at composing an editorial about the wheelchair race, when her part-time secretary brought her the morning mail.

'Someone put this in our box without a stamp,' she said, handing a long, plain envelope to Tish. The letter was addressed simply to 'Miss Holmsworth', with 'Personal' scrawled in capital letters in the lower corner.

'Odd,' Tish said, ripping the envelope open. She unfolded the letter, gasping as she read:

> Dear Miss Holmsworth,
>   I have read Peggy Willson's letter, and will be very happy to be her sponsor. Tell her that I will pay fifty dollars for the first half-mile, one hundred for the second, two hundred for the third, and so on. If she goes all five miles, I'll double the total. The only condition is that I remain anonymous.
>
> > Regards,
> > Nicholas Morgan

'Good lord, have you any idea how much money that would be?' the secretary cried.

'Vaguely,' Tish replied. She jumped up and grabbed her sweater from the hook by the door. 'Hold down the fort for me. I'm going to show this to Peggy, and then to Larry. Will he ever be surprised!'

Peggy, whom Tish caught between classes at the high school, was ecstatic, and happily fell in with Nicholas Morgan's desire to be anonymous. 'That makes it neat and mysterious,' she said. 'If anyone pesters me about who it is, I'll tell them it's a sheikh from some oil-rich kingdom.'

'Good idea,' Tish replied.

Larry, however, was less delighted and less sanguine about the request.

'That kind of money is peanuts to him. And why would the man want to keep his identity a secret? Doesn't he want the people around here to think he has a heart?'

'I think he just doesn't want to flaunt his money,' Tish replied. 'Not many people can afford that kind of donation.'

'So?' Larry shrugged. 'Everyone will guess it was him, anyway.'

'Not necessarily. I'm going to make it sound as if it came from someone very secretive and far away,' Tish said, annoyed by Larry's lack of enthusiasm.

'It won't work,' Larry said, with a superior look that only served to infuriate Tish further. 'You might as well save your literary skills.'

'Larry Johnson,' Tish stormed, 'you are the most complete wet blanket I have ever met! I think it's a fantastically generous offer. And if I have the slightest, the very slightest idea that you have mentioned who it's from, I'll never speak to you again!'

'Now, Tish, calm down,' Larry said, giving her a placating smile.

'Calm down? Why? I'd rather you'd get excited for a change!' Tish retorted, and stalked out of his office.

It was not long before she regretted her ill-temper, and she spent most of the two weeks before the race trying not to repeat her performance. Larry was, after all, a basically nice person. It wasn't his fault that she had become so emotionally involved with a man who wouldn't even speak to her, and it was no wonder that he thought it a bit strange. More than once she thought of telling him what her real dilemma was, but always decided against it. It was, she decided, not only that she feared what Larry's response might be. There was something very personal, very private, about the story she had to tell. It was not something to be bandied about in gossip over the back fence. She would keep it from the rest of the world until Nicholas Morgan himself had heard it, whenever that might be.

The late October Saturday of the race was grey and chilly, but Peggy assured Tish that she preferred it that way.

'The heat really bothers me,' she said, 'but I think I might be able to go the whole five miles today.'

'Don't overextend yourself,' Larry warned.

'No, don't,' Tish agreed, 'but remember that you don't have to win the race to get the sponsor's money. Just keep rolling along.' She watched the start of the race, by the bandstand in the park, then moved along to keep pace, snapping pictures for the paper as she went. When the race was half over, and Peggy was still pushing herself along bravely, she went to the finish line in front of the county court house and got herself in position to get shots of the winners. Several strong male athletes finished in record time, but there were still dozens of younger contestants who were able to go the distance.

'Is Peggy Willson still in the race?' she asked Jeff, who had been running back and forth, reporting on who had dropped out and who had not.

'Yes!' he answered, pointing to the spot where the contestants came into view around a curve in the road. 'Here she comes!'

Peggy, her arms so tired that she could only manage an occasional push, was doggedly proceeding along the route, her face set in grim determination.

'She's gonna make it!' Jeff cried. 'Go, Peggy!'

Peggy looked up and grinned, giving a harder push. Moment by moment, while Tish held her breath, the courageous girl came closer. Tish focused her camera on the finish line. She caught the moment when, with one last push, Peggy came across, her arms raised in victory

and a triumphant smile on her face that delighted the
whole, cheering crowd.

'I did it!' she cried. 'I did it!'

'Bless your sweet heart, you certainly did,' Tish said,
hugging her. 'You were absolutely great. Fantastic! Even
stupendous! Listen, dear, I have to run this film back
to be developed, but I'll see you at the awards ceremony
in a few minutes. Larry will stay here and help you over
to the reviewing stand. You need a rest.' She gave Peggy
another hug. 'I knew you could do it.'

How wonderful, she thought, as she hurried back
down the street towards the *Laketown Herald* office.
Peggy had had the chance to feel like someone really
special again. And all thanks to Nicholas Morgan. She
would have to write him a note and tell him.

'Whoops!' she said, stopping just before she walked
headlong into a tall man who stepped out of a shadowed
doorway in front of her. 'Oh!' she gasped. 'It's you.'
For standing directly before her was, unmistakably,
Nicholas Morgan, wearing a western hat pulled down
low over his brow and mirrored sunglasses. 'Did you see
the finish?' she asked, when she had regained her breath.
'Peggy made it all the way.'

'I thought she would.' He reached into his pocket and
handed Tish a cheque. It was a cashier's cheque, drawn
on a New York bank.

'Yes, I guess you did,' Tish replied, looking first at
the cheque, and then back at her own reflection in
Nicholas Morgan's sunglasses. There was no way that
she could see those clear blue eyes through them, no clue
about what the man was thinking or feeling. Wasn't it
enough that she protect his anonymity, without his hiding
from her even now? She frowned. 'I'd like to thank you,

but those blasted glasses make me feel as if I'm talking to a robot. I hate those things.'

'Bright light is painful for my eyes,' Nicholas Morgan replied.

'It's cloudy today, in case you hadn't noticed,' Tish said, raising her chin and looking at the man through narrowed eyes. 'And I doubt if it would pain you any more than it does me to have to talk to my own reflection.'

Nicholas Morgan made a little coughing sound, almost like a laugh, and removed the glasses. 'You are certainly a very plain-spoken and rather forceful young lady,' he said.

Tish noticed with relief that there was a flicker of amusement in those cool blue eyes. Apparently she had succeeded in getting those glasses out of the way without offending the man. 'I suppose you might say that,' she replied. 'Anyway, now I can thank you properly, and tell you that your sponsorship meant a great deal to Peggy. I think her experience today will go a long way towards convincing her that she's capable of a lot more than she thought before. I wish you'd let her thank you in person.'

'I'm afraid that's not possible,' Nicholas Morgan replied, with a little shake of his head.

'You, sir,' Tish said, giving him a sideways glance, 'are a very stubborn man.' She felt a surge of pleasure when the lines around Nicholas Morgan's eyes crinkled into a little smile, even though his mouth remained sober.

'I suppose you might say that,' he answered. He looked past Tish's shoulder. 'I'd better go before someone comes along. Tell Peggy that I'm very proud of her, will you?'

'Of course,' Tish said. Suddenly she felt almost panicky. Nicholas Morgan was about to disappear once again. 'Wait just a second. I think I got a good picture of Peggy crossing the finish line. Would you like a copy?'

'Why, yes. Yes, I would.' Nicholas Morgan replaced his sunglasses. 'You could leave it with Titus some time when it's convenient.' He started towards an inconspicuous old car parked at the kerb.

'You didn't scold Titus for letting me in before, did you?' Tish asked, in an effort to keep the conversation going a little longer.

Nicholas Morgan paused and looked back. This time the left corner of his mouth was actually quirked upwards in a smile. 'No. I didn't want to find out what kind of item you'd make of that, after listening to your command of adjectives.'

Tish grinned. 'And that was without my thesaurus. Is there some reason that I couldn't bring the picture to you in person?'

'Tish! There you are. Come on. Everyone's waiting for you.'

At the sound of Larry's voice, Tish turned her head to see him bearing down on them at a trot. When she looked back, Nicholas Morgan had already slipped into his car and was starting the engine. Now she would never get an answer to her question, and she had thought it might have been 'no'. She scowled at Larry.

'You certainly picked a devil of a time to make your grand entrance,' she sighed.

CHAPTER THREE

'MY GOD, he's ugly,' Larry said, almost as if he had not heard Tish's remark. Then he scowled, his face as angry as Tish had ever seen it. 'Why is it I suddenly have the feeling you'd rather have a tête-à-tête with that bastard than talk to me?'

For a moment Tish was so taken aback that she could think of no reply. Larry had no right to act so jealously! He had no claim on her, except in his imagination. It was difficult enough, trying to make contact with the most elusive man in the state, without his interfering. Then she saw Larry's wounded look and managed to calm her anger. There was, she admitted to herself with a qualm of guilt, something to what Larry had said, and he was obviously hurt by her thoughtless remark.

'Don't be ridiculous,' she said, although her voice lacked conviction. 'I'm just curious about the man, like everyone else in town. Come on. It will only take me a second to drop off this film. How is Peggy? Is she recovering OK?'

'She's fine, but don't change the subject,' Larry said, jogging along beside Tish as she broke into a run. 'Ever since that damned rock concert, you've acted as if about two-thirds of your mind was on that Morgan character. I don't buy your explanation that it's only curiosity.'

'Larry, let's not talk about it now,' Tish pleaded. She opened the *Herald* door and handed the film to the young man who was waiting there for it, one of the part-time helpers that she hired from the community of college students in order to keep costs on the paper to a minimum. 'Make some extra prints of the picture of Peggy Willson, will you, please?' she asked him. Then she turned and hurried back down the street, Larry still beside her.

'I think it's time we talked about it,' Larry persisted. 'I want you to come to my house for dinner tonight so we can.'

'All right,' Tish agreed. Anything to get him off the topic for the time being! She didn't want his grouchy mood to rub off on her and spoil the moment of triumph for the courageous athletes.

Fortunately, Peggy's brilliant smile was enough to brighten the gloomiest heart, and the applause as she received the cheque from her anonymous benefactor was almost deafening.

'He said to tell you he's very proud of you,' Tish whispered in her ear.

'He saw me?' Peggy asked.

Tish nodded.

'I'm so glad,' Peggy said. 'It makes me sad to think of him being so lonely.'

'Me, too,' Tish agreed. Maybe that, even more than her curiosity about his real character, was the reason she was so determined to make contact with Nicholas Morgan. At least, that was the reason she gave Larry that evening, after he had treated her to his own special dinner of beautifully cooked steaks, accompanied by a lovely salad, baked potatoes, and a wine that definitely did not come from the Morgan Wineries.

'I know you're soft-hearted,' Larry said with a sigh, 'but realistically, Tish, what else can the man do but stay alone? With that face of his, he'd frighten small children.

I wonder what he does when he shows those fancy horses of his. Wear a mask?'

'I don't think he's that ugly,' Tish said, bristling. 'In fact...' she tried to picture Nicholas Morgan, but found it difficult to remember anything but those clear blue eyes '...it's funny,' she went on, 'but when I was talking to him I didn't even notice his scars. I guess he is afraid of what people will think, though. I looked at those stories we've had about the horse shows over the years, and I gathered that he doesn't actually show the horses himself. He breeds and trains them, but someone else rides in the shows.'

Larry shook his head. 'Well, it's a sad story, but I've heard enough about Nicholas Morgan to last me a lifetime. I want to talk about us.' He put his arm around Tish, who was sitting beside him on a sofa, before a cosy fire. 'It's time you made a decision, Tish. I want to get married and have a family before much more time passes, and you should be thinking along those lines, too. How about it? Will you finally accept my proposal? You could come and meet my family at Thanksgiving time, and we could be married at Christmas.'

Tish looked at Larry, a panicky knot forming in her midsection. She studied his smooth, dark hair, his gentle, unlined face, the anxious look in his soft, brown eyes. He was right. It was time she stopped stringing him along. But how could she tell him no, when she knew how much it would hurt him, and how could she say yes, when she still wasn't sure?

'Oh, Larry,' she said, laying her hand along his cheek. 'I...'

'Shhh,' he said, pulling her closer. He took her face in his hands and placed his mouth against hers, kissing her very slowly and deliberately.

Tish tried desperately to feel something of the kind of passion that she thought the kiss of the man she was destined to marry should arouse, but it did not happen, even though she flung her arms around his neck and pressed herself tightly against him. Whether Larry was aware of her failure she was not sure, for he seemed content when she pulled away and said huskily, 'I'm afraid I'm a little tired to make such a big decision tonight. I'll let you know in a week, if that's all right with you.'

'All right,' he agreed. 'One week from now. Same time, same place?'

'Same time, same place,' Tish replied, although the thought of it made her feel still more desperate.

The next day, Tish got her old ten-speed bike out of the garage behind her house and had new tyres fitted. Peggy's remark about having ridden out to Castlemont had reminded her how much she used to enjoy riding out in the country, the wind in her face seeming to clear her mind, and the exercise stimulating her body so that all of its sensations were heightened. She felt a strong need of something to help clarify her thinking, so that she could make the decision that Larry demanded. She did not want to make some muddled, emotional choice that she would later regret. Unfortunately, as she rode farther and farther each evening in the crisp autumn air, her thoughts only became more confused. She would be thinking about all of the positive aspects of a marriage to Larry, when suddenly her mind would switch to Nicholas Morgan. What was he doing? Would he have let her bring the picture if Larry hadn't interrupted them? What a strange, shy little smile he had given her. Was it shy, or was it that he had so little to smile about that

he was out of practice? Or could it be that it hurt him
to really smile?

By Saturday, the day that she had promised Larry to
give him her decision, Tish was in agony, no more ready
than she had been the week before. She got up early,
determined to ride until she either had made a sensible
decision or dropped from exhaustion. The morning was
chilly, so she put on her bright orange insulated
sweatshirt and fastened the attached hood tightly over
her dark curls. Just as she was about to leave, her eyes
fell on the manilla envelope containing the copy of her
picture of Peggy Willson, lying on the countertop by her
telephone. Could she, she wondered, ride as far as
Castlemont and back again? It would be almost twenty
miles. If that wouldn't be enough to serve her purpose,
nothing would.

'What do you think, Rocky?' she asked the cat, who
was finishing his breakfast with noisy gusto. 'I know,'
she answered herself, 'you don't give a darn as long as
I get back in time to feed you your dinner. Well, don't
worry about that. I have to be back. Tonight is the fatal
night.' With that, she picked up the picture, tucked it
inside her jacket and, shooing Rocky ahead of her, went
out of the door.

The first part of the ride was easy, downhill most of
the way. The second part, winding back into the hills,
was quite steep, and Tish was forced to get off and push
her bike several times, panting and beginning to perspire
from the effort, in spite of the chilly day. At last she
saw the beginning of the wall surrounding the Morgan
property. The family must always have had a strong
desire for privacy, she mused, for the brick wall was solid
and a good eight feet tall, topped with a cap of huge
limestone blocks as big as tombstones laid on their sides.

She pumped determinedly up the last incline before the gate, and then jumped off her bike in front of the small brick building in which Titus kept guard of the wrought-iron gates. She knocked on the door, and moments later Titus emerged.

'Well, look who's here,' he said, smiling a warm greeting. 'Since when did Letitia Holmsworth become a cyclist?'

'Since Peggy Willson reminded me what fun it is,' Tish replied. She took the picture from beneath her jacket and handed it to Titus. 'This is a copy of the picture I took of Peggy crossing the finish line the day of the race. Mr Morgan said he'd like a copy, and I was to leave it with you.'

Titus nodded. 'Mind if I have a look?' he asked. 'I saw it in the paper, but the big prints are always better.'

'Go ahead,' Tish replied. 'I think it turned out very well.' She sighed. 'I do wish Mr Morgan would let me give it to him in person. I don't suppose there's any chance you might let me in again?'

'I wouldn't push my luck with Mr Morgan too far,' Titus said, shaking his head. 'He can have a very hot temper. Besides, he's not apt to be at the house. He exercises his horses at this hour.'

'Oh, I see.' Tish bit her lip, the feeling of frustration that Nicholas Morgan's elusiveness always provoked aggravating her own volatile temper. 'I don't suppose he ever lets anyone watch him ride, either,' she grumbled.

'No,' Titus said, tucking the picture back into its envelope. 'That's a mighty fine picture of little Peggy. Bless her heart. That's an awfully nice thing you did for her.' He took off his uniform cap and scratched his balding head. 'You know, the field where Mr Morgan works his horses is right next to the wall, on down about a quarter of a mile.' He jerked his head in the direction past the gate. 'Of course, I couldn't help you any, but there is an old oak tree right next to the wall that isn't hard climbing once you get up into it. I've seen a few of the country boys doing it. I had to chase them down, but I wouldn't need to know you were there.'

Tish grinned. 'Thanks, Titus. I don't know how my tree-climbing is, but I'll give it a try.' She swung herself back on to her bike, and, giving Titus a parting wave, pedalled on down the road.

The oak tree Titus had mentioned was not hard to find, but getting up into it was obviously a problem. The lowest branches were well out of Tish's reach. She got off her bike and studied the problem for a few minutes. Maybe, if she leaned her bike against the tree and stood on the seat, she could reach. She braced the bike as firmly as she could, then climbed up. It was still going to require a little spring, and if the bike fell over she was going to be in a real fix. She stood still, trying to decide if it was worth the risk. Suddenly, from over the wall, the wind flung the sound of horses' hoofbeats, and a man's voice talking to the animal in soothing tones. It was Nicholas Morgan's voice, soft and cajoling.

'Good boy. Come on, now, let's try it again.'

Tish looked up at the branch and measured the distance. It wasn't all that far. She could make it. She bent her knees, sprang upward, and clutched the branch with her fingertips. Quickly she swung her sneakered feet against the tree trunk and walked herself upward, gaining a firmer hold. Shortly she was kneeling on the branch, reaching for the next higher one. When she had gained it, she could see over the wall. What she saw made her catch her breath in sheer admiration. Nicholas Morgan, his broad shoulders encased in a dark leather jacket, was astride a magnificent black horse, racing towards a three-rail jump at top speed. He leaned forward, took the horse over effortlessly, then wheeled and slowed, bending to stroke the horse's neck.

'Good work, big fellow,' he said. He walked the horse for a few minutes, then urged it into a canter again, sweeping around the field in a huge figure-eight, changing leads from time to time.

Enthralled, and wanting to be able to see better, Tish worked her way out the branch to where it hung close to the wall. From there, she carefully stretched one leg out, getting a foothold on the wall and then letting go of the branch.

'Whew!' she breathed, sinking first to her knees and then sitting down cross-legged on the top of the wall. She looked back momentarily and then down, wondering how she was ever going to get off this perch. Oh, well, she'd think of something when the time came. Meanwhile, she was going to sit quietly and watch Nicholas Morgan ride, something, she was sure, not many people were privileged to do. If he saw her... well, she'd worry about that when and if he did. So far, he seemed totally concentrated on what he was doing.

There were several jumps set up of the kind Tish had seen in the steeplechase events she had watched before, but they were not set in a tight pattern as they would be for a race. Apparently, the horse was learning to do them one at a time. And how beautifully he was learning. His movements were like liquid satin, the figure on his back so much a part of him that it seemed they had been sculpted of the same material. Only the burnished copper of Nicholas Morgan's hair stood out in sharp contrast, and the occasional flash of a reflection told Tish that he was again wearing the mirrored sunglasses.

How long she watched, Tish was not sure, but she had no desire to move, in spite of the fact that the top of the wall was cold and hard. It was a revelation to see Nicholas Morgan at work doing something he obviously loved. There was no suggestion of a scarred, embittered man, only the beauty and grace of a skilled athlete. He carried his head with the same arrogant dignity as the animal he rode, bending only to murmur words of encouragement and to stroke the horse's silky neck with a gentle hand. If only, Tish thought, he could see himself as she saw him now, he would never hide from the world again.

At last it seemed the lesson was over. Nicholas rode away from the jump area, across the field, then turned to give the horse one last carefree gallop around the outside edge.

'Uh-oh, he'll see me now,' Tish muttered. She looked back at her tree, then down at the ground so far below. There was no sensible way to get to either one very quickly, without risking some broken bones. She might as well just sit tight and suffer through Nicholas Morgan's wrath. Maybe she could jolly him out of it again. She watched with a quickening pulse as the horse rounded what would have been the far turn on a racetrack, then started back towards her. At what precise moment Nicholas Morgan saw her, she wasn't sure, but suddenly she was aware that horse and rider were coming straight at her at full speed.

'Get down from that wall!' Nicholas Morgan shouted, leaning forward in his saddle. He reached behind him and produced what looked like a small whip. 'Get down from there, or by God I'll knock you down,' he snarled, his voice harsh with rage.

Oh, lord, he doesn't know who I am! Tish thought in a panic as the horse thundered ever closer. In her hooded sweatshirt and jeans, she must look like one of the neighbouring farm boys. Nicholas's arm was extended now, as if he fully intended to knock her from the wall as he rode by. Tish scrambled to her knees and gave a quick assessment of the possibilities of jumping. Outside the wall it was rocky. Inside it was softer, but the horse might either step on her or be so startled that it would panic and throw its rider. There was only one thing to do. She lay down flat, her hands gripping the edge of the limestone slab. The hoofbeats roared even closer, and suddenly Tish felt the sting of something striking her on the bottom.

'Ouch!' she cried. 'You stop that!' She clutched her bottom and pushed herself to a half-sitting position at the same time as Nicholas Morgan reined in his horse and turned back to accost her again.

'Get down from there, you miserable young... Oh, my God.' Nicholas Morgan's words died on his lips. For a moment, as he drew near, his expression was stricken. Then he seemed to regain his determination to be angry. 'Well, well. The ubiquitous Miss Holmsworth,' he said in chilly tones. 'To what do I owe this latest intrusion?'

Tish sat up the rest of the way, pushing her hood back as she did so. She frowned into the reflecting sunglasses. Wasn't the man even going to apologise for swatting her with his whip? It was impossible to tell if he was even sorry, with those blasted glasses in the way.

'Who-wants-to-know?' she asked in a robotlike monotone, planting her hands on her hips and giving the offending glasses a pointedly disgusted look. Her implication was understood, for the glasses were quickly removed with an impatient gesture. 'Ah, Mr Morgan,'

Tish said then, inclining her head graciously. 'How nice to see you again. What a charming welcome.'

Nicholas Morgan had the grace to look slightly embarrassed. 'Obviously, Miss Holmsworth,' he said, 'if I had known it was you I wouldn't have struck you. I'm sorry if I hurt you. However, I don't recall having invited you, and I wouldn't have made the mistake if you weren't dressed like a boy.'

Tish took pity on him. 'I know you didn't know,' she said. 'But you did invite me, in a way. I rode my bicycle out to bring the picture of Peggy. I left the picture with Titus and then rode on. When I heard your voice and the sound of your horse's hooves I stopped and climbed from my bicycle into that tree,' she pointed to the oak behind her, 'and then on to the wall. It's going to be a little tricky getting back to the tree, so I couldn't just jump when you shouted at me. I'll manage it, though.'

'And probably break your neck in the process,' came the dry reply. 'How long have you been there?'

'For quite a long time,' Tish said, watching Nicholas Morgan closely for some clue as to how angry he really was. 'I've never seen such beautiful riding or such a gorgeous horse. It was so thrilling to watch that I couldn't leave. I'm sorry if I've disturbed you.'

Nicholas Morgan's jagged right eyebrow lifted sceptically. The cool blue eyes studied Tish's face intently for a moment, and then narrowed. 'I don't think you're the least bit sorry.'

Tish stared back levelly, a little shiver going through her. There was something different going on behind those dark-fringed eyes, but she was not sure what it was. He was right, of course, but not, it seemed, terribly angry.

'No, I'm not,' she agreed. 'It might even have been worth getting knocked from the wall.'

'That I doubt.' Nicholas Morgan grimaced. For some
time he appeared to be evaluating the situation. 'I
suppose I'll have to help you down on this side,' he said
finally. With that, he swung down from his horse. 'Stand,
Titan,' he said, dropping the reins over the horse's head.
He turned toward Tish. 'Let yourself over the side,
slowly. I'll lift you down as soon as I can reach you.'

While Nicholas Morgan had been hatching his plan,
Tish had been studying his face. Odd, she thought, that
no matter how hard she tried she could not find him
really ugly. There was too much character there, too
much strength and dignity. It was the face of a man she
could not possibly believe to be a coward.

Tish did not waste a second when Nicholas issued his
instructions to get down on his side of the wall. She
scrambled to her knees, then to her stomach, and thrust
herself over the edge. She had not got far when a pair
of strong hands grasped her waist.

'Let go, now,' commanded a deep voice. 'I've got you.
There.' He set her on her feet. 'What's the matter?'

'I think it was riding up those hills,' Tish said, looking
up at Nicholas, while rubbing her wobbly legs. 'I'm not
used to riding so far.' Either that, or it was something
supernatural. The moment those powerful hands had
grasped her, she had felt a surge of dizzyness that seemed
to have settled in her knees.

Nicholas shook his head. 'You should have better sense
than to attempt such a ride if you're not used to it. I
should make you walk back to your bicycle, but . . . raise
your arms up.'

'What for?'

'So I can put you up on Titan, and we can ride back
to the stable. He's not used to carrying double, but you're

so tiny, I don't think he'll mind. Then I'll drive you back to your bike.'

At that announcement, Tish could think of nothing to say, so she obediently lifted her arms, and was quickly whisked into the air and set on to the great horse's saddle. Nicholas Morgan immediately mounted behind her.

'Relax,' he commanded, tucking one arm around her midsection. He made a small clucking noise, and they were off.

It had all happened so fast that Tish felt dazed. The smell of leather, of the horse, and the warm, musky smell of the man so close behind her, blended into an intoxicating combination. The cool air sent Tish's curls flying, and she leaned her head back, breathing deeply, trying to assure herself that this was not a dream. If it was, she thought, it would be wonderful if it would never end.

Nicholas was silent as they crossed the field, followed a small lane past several other fields, then slowed to a trot as they circled around the mansion. He brought Titan to a walk when they approached the gates of the paddock area surrounding a huge stable, which was set quite a distance behind the house.

'Here we are,' he said, stopping the horse with a soft, 'Whoa, boy.' He swung himself down, then looked up at Tish. 'Can you find the stirrup and let yourself down?'

'Sure thing,' Tish said, not wanting to appear inept after her thrilling ride. She looked down and slid sideways, inserting her foot into the stirrup, while Nicholas steadied her with his hand. It was quite a stretch, but she managed to sling her right leg across the horse's back without dragging her foot, then jumped to the ground.

'Very good,' Nicholas commented.

The small compliment sent a warm current through Tish. It was, somehow, quite special that the man would realise how difficult the manoeuvre had been for someone her size.

'Do you ride?' Nicholas asked.

'I used to, a little,' Tish replied. 'Not like you, of course.' She looked around her, at the lovely view of hills beyond and beneath the paddock, the stretches of still green pastures and now barren vineyards. So this, she thought, was Nicholas Morgan's domain. It was somehow fitting that such a magnificent horseman would have such kingly surroundings. A horse whickered from somewhere inside the stable and Titan answered, pawing the ground with one forefoot. Tish was reminded that Nicholas Morgan must have many more marvellous animals.

'How many horses do you have?' she asked.

'Twenty, at the moment,' Nicholas replied. 'There will be more when spring foaling-time comes.'

'Twenty,' Tish echoed, staring toward the stable. When she was younger, she had used to dream of having even one horse of her own. 'I don't suppose I could see them?' she said wistfully, looking up at her tall companion. His immediate frown sent a shaft of cold unhappiness through her and she looked away. Wasn't there anything that he would share, with even one person? She was unprepared when suddenly he seemed to have had second thoughts about his refusal.

'I suppose, as long as you're here...' he said slowly. Tish looked quickly back at him, ready to thank him, only to see him insert his fingers to his mouth and give an ear-splitting whistle. 'Where in the devil is that groom?' He was scowling darkly in the direction of the stables.

A thin young man came hurrying towards them, his eyes almost popping out of his head at the sight of Tish standing beside his employer.

'About time, Stanley,' Nicholas growled. 'This is Miss Tish Holmsworth of the *Laketown Herald*,' he added, as the man kept staring at Tish. 'She's here to do a story about our breeding operation.'

'Yes, sir,' Stanley replied. 'Miss Holmsworth.' He bobbed his head at Tish, then took Titan's reins and led him through the paddock gate.

'That is what you had in mind, isn't it?' Nicholas asked, one eyebrow cocked at Tish, who was staring at him, open-mouthed.

CHAPTER FOUR

'No!' Tish said vehemently. She was about to issue a strong denial, then stopped herself. Did he really think that was why she had climbed his wall, she wondered, or had he convinced himself of that after deciding that she couldn't possibly have had merely an innocent interest in him and his horse? If she told him the truth, that she'd only wanted to talk to him again, he either wouldn't believe her or would misinterpret her motives. He was so sensitive about his appearance that he would assume it was out of morbid curiosity or pity. She had better say something tactful, and at the same time try to take advantage of the unexpected opportunity he was giving her, for whatever reason.

'I mean,' she went on, trying to make the situation bearable for both of them, 'that it wasn't what I had in mind when I left home. It really wasn't.' She smiled. 'But now that I'm here I'd like to very much.' She pulled her empty hands from the pocket of her sweatshirt and held them outstretched. 'I didn't bring any paper or pencils with me.'

'We can remedy that,' Nicholas said, giving no sign as to whether he believed Tish or not. 'Come along.' He led Tish through the gate and into the stable, pausing to take a phone from its hook on the wall. 'Send me down a pad of paper and some pencils,' he said brusquely into the mouthpiece. Then he looked back at Tish. 'It will be here in a minute. Would you like something to eat while we wait?'

'I...er...sure,' Tish replied, still too stunned by this whole turn of events to be very quick in replying. She followed as Nicholas strode across the front of the stable and went into what she thought might be a tack-room. Instead, it was a plain little room, outfitted like a small, efficient apartment. There was a sofa-bed, a table and two chairs, and a miniature kitchen.

'I live down here when the mares are foaling,' Nicholas explained. 'It also saves me having to go back to the house to eat when I'm busy.' He brought out paper plates and silverware, then opened the refrigerator and pulled out several kinds of luncheon meats and cheeses, and set them and a loaf of bread on the table. 'Not fancy, but it will do. Help yourself.'

'Thank you,' Tish said. She felt suddenly nervous, as if in one giant step she had become part of something very intimate to Nicholas Morgan. To hide her feelings, she busied herself making a sandwich and scratched around in her momentarily infertile brain for the kinds of questions she should begin to ask. When the paper and pencils were brought, Nicholas again introduced her to the servant who brought them, as if he were afraid her presence might be misinterpreted. That might well be, Tish thought, but it could do no harm to see if he might unbend a little when no one else was present.

'You make it sound as if my entire name is Miss-Tish-Holmsworth-of-the-*Laketown-Herald*,' she commented when the man had left. She gave Nicholas Morgan a sideways glance. 'My name is Letitia Prudence Holmsworth, but you may call me Tish.'

There was a momentary crinkling of amusement around Nicholas Morgan's strikingly blue eyes that gave Tish another of those little rushes of warmth that any sign of pleasure in his usually stern face produced.

'Thank you, Tish,' he replied. 'You may call me Nicholas.'

'Nicholas,' she said. She smiled impishly. 'I thought you might tell me that I could call you Mr Morgan.'

At that, Nicholas actually chuckled softly. 'Perhaps I should have,' he said. 'I wouldn't want to spoil my image, such as it is.' Then he became very serious again. 'I want it clearly understood,' he said, 'that your story is to be about my horses, and not about me. Not at all. Except when it might be necessary to explain something.'

Tish raised her head and studied the man sitting across the table from her. That was, she thought, exactly what she would have expected him to say. 'I'll do my best,' she replied. 'You may read the story when I'm through with it, if you like.'

'I would like to,' he said, then added, almost as if he were afraid of offending Tish, 'Not that I don't trust you. Only to check and be sure everything is accurate.'

As soon as they had finished their sandwiches, Nicholas took Tish into the stables. She soon felt that, even more than learning about his horses, she was learning something very important about Nicholas Morgan. Gone was the stern, unbending, withdrawn man that everyone thought he was; in his place was a man of warmth and passion. When he began introducing her to his horses, he described the excellence of their particular talents and blood-lines with glowing adjectives. When he spoke of their idiosyncrasies, it was with the fond indulgence of a loving parent. He showed her his meticulous records of the animals' performance, his careful assessments of different feeding rations for the brood-mares and the young colts and fillies. It was obvious to Tish that this was a story that he had wanted to tell for a very long time, and she made voluminous notes, checking and rechecking to be sure she had everything right. At last, Nicholas took her to a field behind the stables where four mares were grazing.

'These mares will be foaling in the spring,' he said. He whistled softly, and a lovely chestnut mare trotted over to him. 'This is Lady Whirlwind,' he said, rubbing the mare's nose and offering her a small bit of carrot from his hand. 'I expect great things from her foal.'

'Is Titan the father?' Tish asked, then grimaced as Nicholas frowned at her. 'Sire,' she corrected herself.

He nodded approvingly. 'Yes,' he answered. 'Together, their ancestors have produced more champions than any other combination you could come up with.' He smiled as the mare nuzzled his shoulder, begging for another treat, and Tish could see that his smile came easily then. There was nothing that kept him from smiling, when his heart was happy. How on earth, she wondered, could she write a story about Nicholas Morgan's horses without something about the passion he felt for them?

She was about to ask him, then thought better of it. She would write the story the way she felt it should be, then let him see it. She might get at least part of what she wanted that way. It would take quite a while to write the story. There was much more she would like to know before she began, if he would let her come again: the history of the Morgan stables, his training procedures, the prizes his horses had won. But even more, she admitted to herself, she would like to see Nicholas again. It touched something deep and fundamental inside her to share his enthusiasm, to see his face change from that of a bitter, lonely man to one of intense pleasure. In the world of Nicholas Morgan, there was no middle ground of cautious grey phrases and clearly marked paths. He was so unlike Larry Johnson.

'Oh, drat!' The phrase slipped out unintentionally, and Tish bit her lip and grimaced as Nicholas turned to look at her questioningly. Why did thoughts of her impending appointment with Larry have to intrude on this perfect afternoon? She glanced at her watch. Four o'clock already. Now she would have to explain her outburst and find out all too soon if she would be welcome again. 'I just remembered I have an appointment this evening,' she said. 'I'd better be going if I'm going to make it back in time.' She felt a shiver go through her once again at the startling clarity of Nicholas's eyes. He seemed to be weighing what she had said very carefully.

'Appointment?' he said finally, raising that one eyebrow in what Tish had already come to realise was a characteristic expression.

He's wondering if that's my euphemism for a date, Tish thought. Well, it definitely was not. For she knew now that her evening with Larry was going to be anything but pleasant. She had to tell him no.

'Appointment,' she said, making a sour face and nodding affirmatively.

'We could put your bicycle in the back of my truck and I could drive you back to town,' Nicholas said. 'That would give you time for a cup of coffee before you leave.'

'I'd like that!' Tish said with enthusiasm, surprised at the invitation. She felt her gloom over the anticipated evening disappear in the warmth of Nicholas's smile, the first smile that he had meant especially for her.

They returned to Nicholas's small apartment in the stables. Tish still felt anxious about asking him if she could return, and so, while he prepared the coffee, she went through her notes again, asking questions to clarify some still sketchy jottings.

'You're very thorough,' Nicholas commented as he brought their coffee and sat down beside her at the small table.

'I have to be when it's a topic I'm not very familiar with,' Tish replied. 'I hate sloppy journalism.' She tapped her pencil thoughtfully against the paper. 'I wonder,' she said, eyeing Nicholas a little apprehensively, 'if I might come back again. I'd like to know about the history of the stables. Perhaps you have some old pictures. And I'd like to learn something of how you go about training your horses.'

Once again, Tish was subjected to a detailed scrutiny, and she felt as if time stood still while she waited for his answer. At last he nodded.

'I think that could be arranged,' he said. 'When would it be convenient? Tomorrow? Or do you have another... appointment?' There was a humorous quirk to his mouth as he said that, as if he did not really believe her statement about the evening.

'Only with my vacuum cleaner and washing machine,' Tish replied, giving him a happy smile, 'and I'd be glad to pass those up. Tomorrow would be fine.' She bit her lip, wondering if she should press her good luck further, then plunged ahead. 'Do you suppose,' she asked, 'that I could watch you ride again?'

This time Nicholas did not hesitate. 'Of course. Come early and I'll demonstrate some of my training techniques for you. Now I'd better take you home. I wouldn't want you to be late for your appointment.'

This time there was an almost teasing note to Nicholas's voice as he said that word, and Tish cast him a knowing glance.

'I know what you're thinking,' she said, 'but you're wrong. It is an appointment, and one I'd just as soon miss.'

Nicholas smiled, but made no further comment. As they drove back to Laketown, he talked inconsequentially about the weather and the autumn colours. Tish asked a few questions about the year's crop of grapes. Something told her that, in spite of Nicholas's willingness to talk about his horses, any personal questions or comments could end this tentative beginning to their friendship. When he had stopped in her driveway and lifted her bicycle from his truck, she held out her hand to him.

'Thank you,' she said formally. 'I really enjoyed this afternoon.'

He took her hand briefly in his. 'So did I,' he said, with an equally formal nod.

Tish gave a little wave as he backed out of her driveway, then quickly turned and wheeled her bicycle into the garage, an indefinable feeling of lightness in her heart. She stood for several minutes in the cool darkness of the little building, savouring the feeling of warmth and strength that had come to her with the clasp of Nicholas's hand, and the pleasant anticipation of seeing him again tomorrow. Then she sighed and, her footsteps dragging, went to open her door. The rest of this day was nothing to look forward to. She had better figure out how she was going to face it.

While she showered and put on a suitable plain skirt and sweater, Tish tried to analyse why she had suddenly become so sure that she must tell Larry no, in order to be better able to explain it to him in the careful, logical terms he would understand. Her effort failed completely. The reason was completely entangled in her day with Nicholas Morgan, and the feeling of excitement he communicated to her. That was a reason Larry would never understand or accept, and she was not sure herself she understood it completely. She was positive, however, that she must not commit herself to life with a man she was fond of, but could never love. Love, she was sure, must contain some of those elements of excitement and passion she found in Nicholas Morgan, elements that were missing from her relationship with Larry. She would simply have to explain to Larry that, while she liked him as a friend, she could not be his wife.

Promptly at seven o'clock, Tish knocked on Larry's door, her nerves steeled for the encounter, and her hopefully tactful speech of refusal carefully rehearsed. She was unprepared for the grim look and the gruff, 'Come in,' with which he ushered her into his house.

'Is something wrong?' she asked as he silently took her coat from her and hung it on his antique hall tree.

'Wrong?' He turned and glared at her, his voice exploding with anger. 'You ask if something's wrong? At least a dozen people saw Nicholas Morgan bring you home this afternoon.'

Oh, the joys of small-town living, Tish thought grimly. 'So what?' she snapped at Larry. 'He was kind enough to give me a story about his horses after I made a fool of myself by climbing on to his wall to watch him ride. It got too late for me to ride my bicycle back to town, so he brought me home. What's wrong with that?'

'So you *admit* you rode out there to see him!' Larry countered triumphantly, as if he had trapped her into confession of a heinous crime.

'I admit nothing of the kind!' Tish cried, infuriated. 'I rode out to take Peggy Willson's picture to Titus. He was the one who told me I could see Nicholas riding if I climbed on to the wall.'

'Oh, so it's Nicholas now, is it?' Larry sneered. 'You certainly work fast.'

Tish stared at him in disbelief. Larry was more aroused now than she had seen him in the several years she had known him, and for a completely ridiculous reason. He had always been mildly jealous, but this was absurd! She gritted her teeth, trying to restrain herself from telling him what a perfect fool he was being. Then she remembered that, since she was doubtless not going to be seeing him after tonight, it did not really matter.

'Yes, it's Nicholas,' she replied calmly. 'And I am going to see Nicholas again tomorrow and get some more material for the story. Whether I'll ever see him again after that, I don't know, but I hope I do, because I like him. But it's really none of your business, because I came here tonight to tell you that, although I like you, too, I can't marry you. Now give me back my coat. I'm going home.'

Larry's face turned pale. 'Now, wait a minute, Tish,' he said. 'I didn't mean to imply I thought you were doing anything wrong. I think it's fine you're able to get a story from that man. Don't make a hasty decision, just because I got on my high horse...'

'It wasn't hasty,' Tish interrupted. 'I thought it through very carefully.' She held out her hand. 'My coat, Larry.'

He ignored her, his face becoming angry again. 'I knew it,' he said, his voice rising as he continued, 'I knew it as soon as you got interested in Nicholas Morgan. You've got some kind of weird emotional hang-up on that miserable, scarred-up devil that has you so confused you can't think straight.'

Tish exploded in anger. 'He is not a miserable, scarred-up devil! He's...' She clamped her mouth shut, afraid she might say far too much if she began, only confirming in Larry's mind his foolish notions. Unfortunately, Larry made the leap alone.

'He's what? A really great guy? Don't make me laugh.' Larry shook his head. 'You'll get over it, Tish, whatever it is. You're an intelligent woman. And I'll still be here when you come to your senses.'

Tish finally walked over and snatched her coat from Larry's hall tree and put it on before he could try to help her. 'I just wish you'd come to yours,' she snapped, jerking open his door. 'I am not going to marry you.'

Larry managed to pat her shoulder as she slipped outside. 'We'll see,' he said.

There was obviously nothing she could say to change his mind, so Tish only gave him a disgusted glance. 'Goodbye, Larry,' she said, and hurried to her car. Was there anything, she wondered, that would make him believe her? If not, he was going to have a very long wait for her senses to return.

The frustration of her encounter with Larry made it difficult for Tish to sleep that night. She hated problems left unresolved, especially when there was no reason for them to be. It was as if all of her efforts to make her decision were for naught. She finally convinced herself that there was nothing further that she could do and went to sleep, awaking in the morning with the satisfaction of having an all too short dream of riding across an endless meadow with Nicholas, on a horse that flew like the wind.

Tish had no appropriate eastern-style riding boots, but she did have some fine old western boots her father had brought her from Texas. They would be better than

sneakers, she decided, for her date to see Nicholas in
action. She buffed them to a glowing shine, and wore
them with her jeans and a heavy turquoise-blue sweater,
well aware that she chose the sweater to bring out the
colour of her eyes. Why not? she defended herself. She
wanted Nicholas to think that she was pretty, although
she wasn't sure that he had any interest in her
appearance.

She was overwhelmingly aware of his appearance when
he greeted her at the paddock gates. He was dressed
exactly as the day before, his black knee-high boots
glistening, his tan, whip-cord riding trousers taut across
his muscular thighs, and the cordovan leather jacket soft
and supple upon his broad shoulders. The copper of his
hair flashed highlights of gold in the early sun, and his
smile, as he greeted Tish, was warm and friendly. He
was, Tish realised in that instant, still an extremely
handsome man, his scars no more relevant to his total
appearance than a speck of dirt on a painting by
Rembrandt.

'Good morning, Tish,' he said, in that deep voice that
Tish found very appealing.

'Good morning, Nicholas,' she replied, taking her cue
from him and maintaining a reserved, although easy,
formality. 'It's a beautiful day.'

'Yes, it is,' he agreed.

His eyes met Tish's, and for a moment she saw an
almost palpable hunger in them before he deliberately
turned his head and looked out across the valleys below,
where an overnight frost was vaporising into a veil of
mist as the sun penetrated to them.

'I think it's going to be quite warm today,' he said.

The note of strain in his voice, added to what she had
seen in his eyes, told Tish that he was very aware of her

as a woman, and was determined not to let it affect him. It would, she decided, behove her to be decorous and proper, and not add to his discomfort. That was not going to be easy, given that she had never been more aware of a man's sexual appeal.

At that moment, Stanley appeared, leading a dainty grey mare across the paddock. Nicholas opened the gate and took the reins from him.

'Good morning, Miss Holmsworth,' Stanley said, smiling shyly, before he turned and retreated again toward the stables.

'Good morning, Stanley,' Tish replied. She looked up at Nicholas. 'You're not riding Titan today?'

'Oh, yes,' he said. 'This is Alyssia. She's for you to ride.'

'For me?' Tish squeaked, any attempts at decorum and propriety lost in her excitement. She had never dreamed that she might get to ride one of Nicholas's beautiful horses.

Nicholas chuckled. 'For you. I thought, since the training I do involves the rider as much as the horse, it would be the best way to demonstrate. Here. Mount up.' He led the horse in front of Tish. 'Alyssia is very gentle,' he added, as Tish hesitated momentarily.

'I just hope she's ready to cope with a real greenhorn,' Tish said as she swung up into the saddle and settled herself. 'I wouldn't want to undo all you've taught her already.'

'There's no chance of that,' Nicholas said confidently. 'She'll be teaching you in no time.' He checked Tish's hold on the reins. 'Just relax,' he said prying loose her death-grip and then patting her hands comfortingly. 'We won't do anything you're not ready for, and if you want to stop, just say "whoa". She understands that.'

'Yes, sir,' Tish said meekly. How she was going to achieve relaxation she could not imagine. She was not only thrilled to be riding, but felt an ever-increasing compulsion to devour Nicholas with her eyes.

Then Stanley brought out Titan, his black coat shining in the sunlight. Nicholas mounted and moved ahead. He looked back over his shoulder and smiled encouragingly.

'Here we go,' he said.

As soon as the horses were in motion, Tish's nervousness vanished. As Nicholas urged Titan into a slow canter, the crisp autumn air flew by Tish's cheeks, ruffling her hair and making her feel as if she were reliving her dream. As soon as they reached the field where Tish had watched Nicholas the day before, he had her dismount. He became totally professional as he then began with the most elemental commands, teaching her to mount and dismount, showing her the perfection he demanded from both horse and rider. He first illustrated and then had her try the different gaits, complimenting her when she did well and correcting her gently when she did not. Later, he took Titan through the elements of jumping while Tish watched, awed at his skill and the communication he had established with his horse. Finally, the morning over, they circled the field, although not at the speed which Nicholas had used the day before when he threatened to knock Tish from his wall.

Once back at the paddock, they turned the horses over to Stanley, who did not have to be whistled for this day.

'You could become an excellent rider,' Nicholas said to Tish, as Alyssia was led away.

Tish smiled, as breathless at the compliment as if she had won an Olympic gold medal.

'Thank you,' she said, 'but I think your horse did most of the good work.'

Nicholas shook his head. 'I know talent when I see it,' he said reprovingly. 'Shall we have some lunch now?' he went on. 'I've arranged to have it at the house. I thought you deserved something better than pot-luck at the stables for your efforts. Then, after that, I can show you some of the family scrap-books. I think the kind of historical material you're looking for will be there.'

'That sounds marvellous,' Tish replied. 'Just let me get my writing materials from my car.' She retrieved her shoulder-bag and notebook, and then followed Nicholas into the mansion, past the armoured figure at the foot of the stairs, and into a room Tish knew immediately from pictures she had seen was the famous Castlemont library. It was two storeys high, with a mezzanine floor running around three sides, and completely lined with books. On the first floor it was furnished with red leather chairs, deep red oriental rugs, and a huge oak table. Two places had already been set at the table with beautiful china and crystal.

'This is a magnificent room,' Tish said, still gazing about her in awe as Nicholas helped her into her chair.

'It's one of the few really liveable-in rooms in this place,' Nicholas said as he took his seat. 'Castlemont was created for a different age.'

'Wouldn't it be fascinating,' Tish said, 'to travel back in time and see it? I'd like to visit, but I don't think I'd want to stay.'

Nicholas agreed, and while they lunched on lobster salad and a fine Morgan wine, they discussed the merits of different periods of history. All the while, Tish had the feeling of a tension building inexorably between them. It was not from what they said, but rather from the pauses between comments, the glances, the motions to emphasise a point. Tish was almost relieved when the luncheon things were removed and she could turn her attention to making notes on the events of the morning, although she felt the notes quite unnecessary. She was sure the entire morning was burned indelibly into her memory.

While Tish was writing, Nicholas went to the shelves and brought out several large volumes. When she had finished and looked up at him, he carried them over to her and then moved his chair close to hers. For a moment, Tish was so undone by his nearness that she could scarcely comprehend what she was looking at, but she gave herself strict orders to get her emotions under control. Things were going too well for her to botch them up by falling apart now. A few more days, and she might actually be able to talk about more personal things with Nicholas. If there were to be more days.

With that hope in mind, Tish directed her attention to the books. There were faded photographs from a century before, showing the building of Castlemont, the stables rising at the same time. Some of the older buildings were no longer present, a huge pavilion for horse-shows having burned at the turn of the century. There were dozens of pictures of horses, charts of lineages, records of achievements, from the earliest days until almost the present. But, when the time for young Nicholas to appear on the scene approached, Nicholas abruptly closed the last book.

'You've already seen the records of what I've done,' he explained.

Tish wondered whether it was that, or because he could not bear to look at the pictures of himself as a happy youngster, with his proud parents still alive, for Nicholas's face was suddenly as closed as the book before him.

Nicholas rose to return the books to the shelves, and Tish sensed that their interview was over. She closed her notebook and put her pen away, brooding over whether she should mention any further contact or leave that to Nicholas. When he turned back toward her, his face still impassive, she stood up.

''I . . . I really appreciate everything you've done,' she said tentatively.

'It's been my pleasure,' he replied. 'I hope your story turns out well.'

That statement, Tish thought, was discouragingly final-sounding. She gathered her courage.

'I think it will,' she said. 'It would be a great help if you'd go over it with me before I'm finished. After I see what other questions come up.' Her heart sank as Nicholas frowned, then jerked his head firmly in a negative response.

'I'd rather not do that,' he said, moving towards her. 'I don't want to see you again. The only reason I let you come at all is because I wanted you to understand that I want to be alone, here, with my horses. They don't care what I look like, they don't give a damn what anyone thinks of me. I enjoy their company. I don't want anyone else's.' He looked directly at Tish for a moment. 'I especially don't want anyone's pity,' he said.

Nicholas's final remark was like a splash of cold water, rousing Tish from the stunned unhappiness that his earlier words had brought.

'I don't recall offering you any,' she snapped. How Nicholas Morgan could interpret anything she had ever done in his presence as pity was beyond her comprehension! Besides that, she knew perfectly well that his only intention had not been simply to convince her that he wanted to be alone. 'And,' she added, her eyes flashing, 'I don't like being lied to.' She shouldered her bag and tucked her notebook under her arm. 'Have a nice life, you and your horses,' she said, whirling and heading for the door, blinking back the hot tears that had sprung to her eyes.

'Wait, Tish.' Nicholas's voice was deep and hollow-sounding.

Tish stopped and turned around.

'Come back here a minute?' he asked softly. He was standing by the table, leaning against it as if he needed support. His expression was troubled, but not angry.

Tish approached him and stood directly in front of him. 'Was there something else you wanted to say?' she asked tightly, feeling tremors of emotion washing through her from Nicholas's intense stare. He nodded, seemingly trying to compose himself.

'You're right. I wasn't entirely honest about why I don't want to see you again,' he said finally. 'I shouldn't have insulted your intelligence and perceptiveness like that.'

'Oh?' Tish raised her eyebrows, at the same time clenching her hands tightly around her notebook. She waited, the tension building almost unbearably inside her, for what Nicholas might have to say now.

'Yes.' Nicholas studied his hands, knotted together in front of him, for a moment, then raised his head and looked directly at Tish, the depth of emotion communicated by his gaze almost palpable in the small space between them. 'It's not that I didn't enjoy your company yesterday and today. I did. You're intelligent, and charming, and spirited... everything I could admire in a woman. But...' his voice became low and husky, 'you are also a very beautiful woman, and I am a very... disfigured man. I could never hope to appeal to a woman like you, and yet you arouse in me every normal male instinct. I long to touch you, to hold you, to kiss you, to possess you in every way a man can possess a woman. Having you near me is torture, and I am not willing to undergo such torture. Nor, even if you could bear the sight of me, could I stand to subject you to the taunts that would go with associating with someone who is not only physically imperfect, but morally flawed. You've heard the story, I know you have, of my cowardice. It is enough that I must live with it for ever. I can't ask someone else to do so. But, when I look at you, I know that very soon there would be nothing else I would want so much as to have you with me for ever, and that it could never be. And so, Miss-Tish-Holmsworth-of-the-*Laketown-Herald*, that is why I must never see you again.'

In the silence that fell after Nicholas's speech, Tish could hear the pounding of her own heart so clearly that she was sure Nicholas could hear it too. In her wildest dreams, she would never have imagined hearing the words she had just heard from Nicholas Morgan. It was a soliloquy, one he must have composed as he tried to explain to himself why he must send her away. The words were so carefully chosen. They were wonderful, totally unexpected words, words that almost spoke of love, almost spoke of marriage. That was startling enough, but Tish was not sure how seriously they were meant. It was, perhaps, only a way of impressing her with the seriousness of Nicholas's argument against their meeting again. The most important, and most aggravating, feature was that the words spoke on her behalf before she had a chance to reply, and said goodbye for ever, not asking for one moment what she wanted or how she felt. She did not think him ugly and disfigured, and, in

spite of his own conviction, she would have bet her own
life that he was not a coward. But how, unless she could
gain his trust, could she convince him otherwise? Her
story of a momentary encounter with a man named
Charlie would not hold much water with a man who was
so sure that he was a coward. And, if she let him tell
her goodbye for ever, she would have no chance to gain
that trust.

Desperately, Tish cast about in her mind for some way
to convince Nicholas that he was on the wrong track.
Should she argue with his viewpoint, or try to present
her own? He had seemed to like her forceful response
before. It was worth another try.

'That was a very nice speech,' Tish said, trying to look
as directly at Nicholas as he had at her, 'but I'm afraid
it doesn't impress me quite as you had hoped it would.
You think you're being noble, but I think you're being
arrogant. What makes you think you can decide what
I'm supposed to think and what I'm supposed to want?
You say that I'm intelligent, but you seem to assume
that I'm incapable of thinking for myself. That I'm too
stupid to know that life is not always a bed of roses, or
so shallow that I would never choose anything difficult
when something easy was available. And you...you seem
so wrapped up in self-pity and a million misconceptions
about what the whole world thinks of you...'

'Stop it, Tish!' Nicholas grasped her face tightly in
his hand and bent so close that his breath was warm
upon Tish's lips as he spoke. 'I wasn't belittling your
intelligence in any way, but, believe me, I understand
what must be far better than you can. I wasn't being
noble. Look at this face. Think about what you know

about me. Can you honestly say you could ever consider marrying me?'

Tish jerked her head free, staring at Nicholas. Did he actually want her to marry him, or was he only trying to validate his own conviction that she would not? If it was the latter, she was not going to let him get away with it. 'Do you really want to marry me?' she asked. 'Is that a proposal?'

'Well,' Nicholas said, looking down uncomfortably, 'I think it was more a question of...'

'Aha!' Tish pointed an accusing finger. 'You are only trying to prove that you're right without asking a single relevant question.'

'All right.' Nicholas reached over and took hold of Tish's hand. 'I'll ask you the most relevant question of all. Letitia Prudence Holmsworth, will you marry me? And don't ask if I mean it. I do.'

That, Tish thought wryly, was certainly calling her bluff. 'I'm not sure,' she replied, her fingers curling tightly around the warmth of his large hand. 'I don't know you well enough yet, just as you don't really know me well enough to ask. But I can tell you right now that I like the way you look, and that something that happened a long time ago is not important to me at all. Nor is what other people think. What would matter most is what kind of a man you are now. And whether I loved you.' She held her breath, watching a myriad of lights flickering deep in Nicholas's eyes as they wandered over her face.

'And you think I ought to give you a chance to find out?' he asked, laying his hand alongside Tish's cheek. 'Even if in the end your answer is no and it breaks my heart?'

'It might be worth the risk,' Tish answered.

Nicholas smiled wryly. 'It might. But, you see, I'm a coward. I'm afraid to take that risk. Goodbye, Tish.' He released her hand and removed his other hand from her cheek.

Tears sprang to Tish's eyes. The warmth of Nicholas's hand was still on her cheek, and through the blur of her tears she could see the soft curve of his lips. She did not want to part from him like this. He had said he wanted to kiss her. What would it be like to be kissed by a man who, after so short an acquaintance, could impulsively ask her to marry him, even though she was sure he knew her answer would be no? She must at least know what it would be like to kiss him, to be held in his arms.

'Are you even afraid to kiss me goodbye?' she asked. When he did not answer, she dropped her bag and notebook to the floor, then took his face between her hands and pulled him very gently towards her, raising her face to his. For a moment he resisted, then with a deep groan he let her have her way, his arms enfolding her as their lips met.

From the moment that their lips touched, Tish knew that she had found something in Nicholas's arms that she had never experienced before. Electricity, chemistry, whatever it was called, it was a powerful force that seemed to flow between them. The warmth of his mouth was both soothing and intoxicating, like a heady liquor that sent flashes of wild colour fleeting before her still wide-open eyes, making her press closer, begging for more and more. Nicholas's eager response, the tender movements of his tongue against her lips, the hands that touched her so gently but so clearly wanted to explore her body, gave Tish a delight that made her heart sing.

He wasn't really afraid of her at all, and he did really want her. She could tell when, with one strong arm, he pressed her body against him and moved to satisfy his increasing desire. She could tell when his hand crept beneath her sweater and sent shivers of longing coursing through her with fingers that delicately touched her bare breast. She let him push her sweater upwards, arching her body so that his lips could feast on the rosy peaks his fingers had found. She gave a soft 'mmmmm' of pleasure, her hands caressing his silky, coppery hair, cradling his head lovingly against her. Never before had she felt so completely transported, so totally focused on nothing but delicious sensations. Surely, Nicholas must be feeling the same strong desires? Surely, now, he wouldn't send her away? A beginning like this must be a signal that more good would come of their being together. But suddenly he stopped and raised his head, and the wild look in his eyes sent a cold terror through Tish's heart.

'What's wrong, Nicholas?' she asked, hurriedly pulling her sweater back down as he thrust her away from him and passed his hand over his eyes in a gesture of despair.

'I'm a fool, that's what's wrong,' he said harshly. 'A coward and a fool.' He glared at Tish. 'Why couldn't you leave me alone? Why did you have to come meddling into my life? Get out. Now! And don't ever try to see me again. I don't want to be responsible for what may happen if you do.'

Being so coldly jolted out of her euphoric state sent Tish's temper flaring.

'Don't worry, you won't have to,' she snapped. 'I thought something wonderful was happening, but I guess I was wrong.' She scooped up her things, ran to the door and jerked it open, turning to give Nicholas one last glare. 'Goodbye!' she said, then slammed the door behind her as hard as she could and bolted across the hall. She did not want that blasted Nicholas Morgan to see the tears streaming down her cheeks!

CHAPTER FIVE

TISH drove home, scarcely able to see through the veil of tears that poured from her eyes. She careened into her driveway, startling Rocky, who leaped straight into the air, his back arched.

'I'm sorry, baby,' Tish said, picking him up and hugging him, and then letting herself into her house. She flung her things on to a chair and then sat down at the kitchen table and buried her face in her arms. A great, nameless ache pervaded her entire body. Why, oh, why was Nicholas so determined to shut her out of his life? Was there nothing she could do to make him see things differently? That thought brought back memories of her failure with Larry and her sobs returned anew. Was there something wrong with Letitia Prudence Holmsworth that made it impossible for men to believe her? Why did the wrong one persist in wanting her to stay, and the one who might be the right one persist in wanting her to go?

'It's crazy, that's what it is,' Tish said, grabbing a large towel and mopping at her face. She looked down as Rocky gave a disgruntled yowl by her feet. 'How would you like it,' she said to him bitterly, 'if I threw you out in the cold just because I was afraid you might interrupt my life?'

She got up and gave the cat a dish of food, watching as he limped to her side and began purring.

'I guess it's lucky you never knew you were different,' she said with a sigh. 'You might not have believed I could love you.'

She sat down again and stared into space, remembering the exciting two days she had spent with Nicholas Morgan. Even if she never saw him again, she thought, he had given her one great gift. He had shown her the kind of passion and intensity she wanted in a man. If she never saw him again ... Deep inside, she still did not believe that could be true.

She muddled through the next day at the newspaper office, unable to keep her mind on one track for more than a few minutes, visions of Nicholas talking, smiling, riding, coming between her and her work as if someone were controlling a projector in her brain. She had just returned home, determined to get herself under better control, when Titus appeared at her door.

'Mr Morgan asked me to deliver this to you,' he said, handing Tish a long envelope.

'Thank you, Titus,' Tish said, looking at the envelope curiously. Could Nicholas have had second thoughts? She felt a little flush of hope. Titus was still standing there. 'Were you supposed to wait for a reply?' she asked.

'Well, no, Letitia,' Titus said, looking slightly embarrassed. 'I just wanted to tell you that I think Mr Morgan really likes you. It's very unusual for him to invite someone to come and see his horses and all. I don't recall his ever doing that before.'

Tish nodded. 'I know. I like him, too. Wait there a minute, will you? I might want to send him a message.'

She went inside and tore the envelope open with trembling fingers, pulling out a sheet of ordinary notepaper, folded in thirds.

'Dear Tish,' she read, 'I'm sorry I made you so unhappy last night, but, believe me, it's better this way. Yours, Nicholas.'

'Better!' Tish cried aloud. She quickly tore a sheet from her own notepad and scribbled on it, 'Dear Nicholas, No, it isn't! Yours, Tish.' She found an envelope, stuffed her note into it, and then took it to Titus. 'Would you please deliver this to Mr Morgan?' she asked. 'And if you can find a brick, hit him with it for me!'

'My, my,' said Titus, looking bewildered. 'Is that all?' he asked, peering at Tish.

'That's all,' she replied.

When Titus had gone, she went back inside and stared at Nicholas's note again.

'Better!' she repeated, frowning. Did the idiot think that, if he kept telling her that, she would believe it? She wadded the letter into a ball and threw it violently across the room. Almost as soon as it hit the floor, she jumped to her feet and retrieved it, straightening the paper once again and then placing it on the table and smoothing it over and over. It was, after all, the only personal remembrance she had from Nicholas. What fascinating, bold handwriting he had, slashing across the page at an angle, with total disregard for the lines on the paper. And what did he mean, 'yours'? If he was hers, why wasn't he here, instead of in that cold mausoleum of a mansion, or in that bare little room in his stables? At that she burst into racking sobs, only stopping when Rocky began playing in such an antic way with one of the damp Kleenex that she dropped that she could not help paying attention to him.

'You're a regular clown, Rocky,' she said to the cat, who turned a complete somersault after a wild leap at the little ball of paper. 'Nothing ever gets you down, does it? I guess maybe I should take a lesson from you. There must be something more constructive I can do besides sit here and blubber. I might as well start on that story. Between that and all of the extra material we'll have for the newspaper for the holiday season, I ought to be able to keep my mind off Nicholas Morgan, the unwilling suitor. If he doesn't want me around, he doesn't want me around. Period. Accept it. I'm the one who wouldn't let him get by with a nice, simple explanation. I'm the one who made him kiss me. It's really all my fault I'm feeling so rotten. Now, what do I do to get over it, hmm?'

The answer to that question continued to elude Tish. She received no more notes from Nicholas, who apparently still thought he knew what was best. Day after day she went through her routine at the newspaper, then returned home to work on her story about Nicholas's horses by night. All the while she felt as if she were only a shell, going through the motions. The least little thing would set off her temper, and it seemed that she spent half of her time apologising to her staff for being unreasonable. Larry, apparently encouraged by the fact that she was not seeing Nicholas regularly, began inviting her out again. She brusquely refused, hoping that he would begin to believe that she had really meant it when she said she would not marry him without her having to go through another scene with him. One more scathing remark about Nicholas from Larry, and she would doubtless flare up like a skyrocket, and reveal too much of what she felt about Nicholas. For, the more she worked on her story, the more she felt drawn to the man on a different level from the overwhelming electricity of their kiss. Everything she remembered from her days with him told her that this was a man of great passion and devotion, one who would give his life to save another, as the man Charlie had thought he had. She simply must get close enough to him to find out what had happened to make him believe he had failed his men so terribly. It just did not seem possible that Mike O'Hara's story was correct.

When the Thanksgiving holiday was only a week away, Tish got a call from Mavis.

'Come and have Thanksgiving dinner with us,' she invited. 'Mom's cooking a huge turkey, and the whole gang will be here. There's no point in you sitting home alone with a TV dinner, now that you and Larry aren't going together.'

'I'll think about it and let you know, OK?' Tish replied. As soon as Mavis had said 'alone', she had pictured Nicholas, alone in that huge house, while all over the town and countryside families were gathering together. If only the man weren't so blasted stubborn, she would gladly cook him a Thanksgiving turkey!

She was brooding about that the next Saturday, while staring at the refrigerated case full of frozen turkeys in the supermarket.

'Going to cook a bird, Letitia?' said a familiar voice in her ear.

'Oh, hello, Titus,' she replied. 'No, I'm afraid not. One of these would last me until spring.' She watched as Titus examined several birds, and then picked up a twenty-pounder. 'You must be having quite a spread,' she said. 'Does Mr Morgan give you Thanksgiving Day off?'

Titus smiled and nodded. 'Oh, yes. He gives the whole staff the day off.'

Tish frowned. 'Then he doesn't have a turkey dinner?'

'No. He says he doesn't want one. He'd rather spend the day cleaning the stables or doing something useful, instead of overeating.'

I'll just bet he would, Tish thought. He loved his horses, but somehow it was very easy to picture him at the head of a kingly table, surrounded by friends and children, smiling as he dispensed large helpings of the festive bird.

For several days, that vision haunted her. There was, of course, no way she could make it become a reality, but she might be able to at least see that he got a decent dinner. He might just send her packing, but it was worth a try. If she didn't see him again soon, she was going to go out of her mind. The previous evening she had found herself typing 'Nicholas' over and over again until a whole page was filled. However, before she made any elaborate plans, she needed to find out from Titus if the gates were left locked or unlocked. There was no way she could climb over the wall with a basket full of turkey and other goodies.

'Well,' Titus said when she stopped to see him at the gate-house, 'I probably shouldn't be telling you this, but they are unlocked. It's a fire regulation, you see. If there's no one here to open them, they must be. Of course, you have to know how to open them.'

'Well, how do you?' Tish said impatiently. When Titus hesitated, she frowned. 'For heaven's sake, Titus, all I want to do is bring Mr Morgan some turkey. If he tells me to go away again, I will.'

Titus looked at Tish knowingly. 'You really like Mr Morgan, don't you, Letitia?'

'Yes,' Tish replied. 'I really do.'

Titus smiled. 'So do I, and I think he needs to see a nice young lady like you. Look here. All you have to do is press this button underneath the window-ledge.' He demonstrated and the gates swung open. 'Do you want to see Mr Morgan now?'

The temptation was great, but Tish shook her head. 'No, I'll wait. It's only two days, and if I go in now, he may get angry and then I'll be afraid to come back. Thank you, Titus. I won't tell him how I found out. I'll tell him I just started pushing and poking at things until they opened.'

That problem solved, Tish hurried back to town to purchase the necessary ingredients for a grand, if not terribly large, feast. She would make turkey with sage dressing, sweet potatoes, cranberry relish, and a mince-meat pie.

On Thanksgiving morning, Tish got up early in order to have everything ready by noon. She kept peering anxiously out the window. A blizzard warning was out for the entire Finger Lakes region, and snow had begun to fall at daybreak. With the wind whipping the snow about, the road to Nicholas's house would drift shut quite early.

She put in an early phone call to wish her father a Happy Thanksgiving, feeling guilty at telling him she was going to the Greers' for dinner. She knew, however, that he would not only consider her plan for the day an invasion of Nicholas's privacy, but foolhardy as well. It was definitely a case of what he didn't know wouldn't hurt him.

As soon as the turkey was ready, Tish packed it and the rest of her preparations into a large, insulated picnic basket and started out, leaving Rocky an extra ration of food in case she did not make it back that night. What Nicholas might think if she were marooned with him, she did not dare to contemplate.

With the wind coming mostly from the northwest, the road was still passable, but the snow was coming so thick and fast that Tish could barely see ahead of her, even with her car lights on. It was with great relief that she finally found the gates of Castlemont in sight. The gates swung open at her touch of the button. The pine sheltered drive was still quite clear, but the moment she gained the clearing at the top of the hill, the windswept snow was blinding. The huge, castle-like mansion was a grey, ghostly shape, a drift across the drive in front of the steps ending her progress once and for all.

'Lord, I hope Nicholas is at the house,' Tish muttered, as she struggled up the snow-banked stairs, slipping and falling once when she missed a step completely. She rang the doorbell, then banged on the door, but no one came. 'You'd think some of the servants would live in and be here,' she grumbled aloud. But maybe, even if they did, they took advantage of the chance to get away from the depressing place. There was nothing for her to do now but to try and make her way to the stables.

She skirted the house, stumbling through the deep snowdrifts, barely able to tell which way she was going. The snow was now falling in icy pellets that stung her face, and she was very glad that she had worn her heavy parka, with wool slacks and a turtle-necked sweater beneath. She found the corner of the house and struck out in what she hoped was the direction of the stables, a direction that was straight into the wind. For what seemed like an eternity she inched forward, hoping that she would soon come to something, even a fence, that would tell her where she was. Stories of people lost out in a blizzard, freezing to death only a short distance from safety, began to prey on her mind. She took a slightly different tack, thinking that she had seen some kind of a shadowy shape ahead of her. The basket was getting so heavy now that she could scarcely hold on to it, and the wind seemed determined to wrench it from her grasp.

'I can't even see,' she sobbed, wiping desperately at her eyes with a mittened hand. The tears from the wind had frozen on her lashes, and they were sticking together. She stumbled, then pitched forward, the basket flying from her hands. The basket disappeared from sight, then hit something solid with a cavernous thump. 'I've found it!' Tish cried aloud, crawling forward on her knees. She could see a light ahead of her as a door opened.

'Nicholas!' she screamed into the wind.

'What in the devil...good lord in heaven! Tish!' Nicholas loomed into view and gathered Tish up in his arms. 'What in God's name are you doing here?' he demanded, peering into her face as he carried her quickly inside his stable-room and closed the door with a kick.

'I'm the good Thanksgiving fairy,' Tish replied through chattering teeth, trying to smile. 'Did you find the basket?'

'Was that what hit my door?' He shook his head as Tish nodded. 'Just a minute.' He set Tish down carefully on a chair, then went outside again, returning with the basket. 'What's in here?' he asked, setting the snow-covered basket on the floor. 'It weighs a ton.'

'Turkey and dressing, sweet potatoes, cranberry relish, mince pie, and some other stuff to nibble on,' she replied.

Nicholas shook his head again, frowning, then turned his back to Tish, his head down and his hands thrust deep in his pockets.

He looks terrific from the back, Tish thought, admiring his broad shoulders and slim hips in the heavy sweater and jeans he was wearing. She began to peel off her own snow-caked jacket.

Nicholas whirled around suddenly. 'Tish, I thought I made it clear...'

'You made a lot of things perfectly clear,' Tish interrupted, 'but I decided to ignore them and come anyway, so just skip the lecture.'

'You can't stay,' Nicholas said, frowning at the sight of Tish removing her coat.

'Yes, I can,' she replied defiantly. 'I barely made it through. My car's stuck in a drift in front of your house. I'd never make it back so you're stuck with me. Where shall I put my coat and boots? They're going to thaw all over your floor.' She handed them to Nicholas, who took them from her with a tight-lipped grimace, hung the coat on a hook near the small wood stove which heated the room, and placed her boots on a rug just inside the door. Then he silently walked over to the window and stared out at the opaque whiteness of the driving snowstorm.

Tish got up and went to the same rug and spent a few minutes trying to brush the snow from her slacks. 'I'm afraid I'm going to be a little damp for a while,' she said with a sigh. She picked up the picnic basket and carried it to the rug to brush off its remaining snow, then placed it on the table. 'Do you have something I could mop up with?' she asked, indicating the puddle the picnic basket had left. She cocked her head, looking sideways at Nicholas, who had gone to sit on the sofa and was staring at her as if in a trance. 'Nicholas?' she queried.

'What? Oh, over there.' He pointed toward the refrigerator, and Tish saw a mop, leaning against the wall.

She mopped up the water, then rinsed the mop and returned it to its position. Nicholas had watched her for a while, but when she again sat in a chair, he had leaned forward and buried his face in his hands. An unhappy ache invaded Tish's heart. She shouldn't have come, after all. He really didn't want to see her. All of his noble, romantic words had just been an excuse to get rid of her. She sat and stared at the shining copper hair, wondering morosely if it might not be better to have frozen in the snow. If only she could think of something to say, but at the moment she was too afraid of what Nicholas might respond to even begin a conversation.

At last Nicholas raised his head, pushing his hands apart across his brow as if to smooth away his frown. He looked at Tish and smiled wryly. 'And just when I was beginning to think that I could get along without seeing you again,' he said.

The weight instantly lifted from Tish's heart. 'Sorry to disappoint you,' she said. 'I never had any such illusions.'

Nicholas got up and flung himself across the other chair backwards as if it were a horse, leaning one elbow on the chair back, his chin on his hand. He reached out with his other hand and placed it over the hand which Tish was resting on the table. 'You could have been killed out in that storm,' he said, his eyes dark with worry. 'Promise me you'll never do such a fool thing again.'

The warmth from Nicholas's touch had raced through Tish and removed the last vestiges of her chill. She looked down at his hand upon hers, and turned her own hand so that she could take hold of his. She flicked a sideways glance at him.

'Then don't make it so blasted hard for me to see you,' she said. She felt Nicholas's fingers tighten around hers.

'I won't,' he said. He cleared his throat and raised his eyebrows, a twinkle of mischief in his eyes now. 'Does this mean that you've decided to marry me?'

So he was going to try to make light of that, Tish thought. It was probably a good idea, given the circumstances. She shook her head, giving him an equally playful look.

'No, it means I've decided to study the question very carefully. I suggest you probably ought to do the same. After all, you don't even know if I can cook. Of course, since you doubtless already have a cook, that particular skill may not be required.'

'Ah, yes.' Nicholas looked at the picnic basket. 'Is there actually a roast turkey in there?'

Tish nodded. 'The real thing. Probably a bit bruised by now, and getting cold.'

'We'll have to find out immediately,' Nicholas said, getting up again and going to retrieve some dishes from the cupboard. 'If you were to marry me, I'd naturally fire the cook. I've always felt a woman's place was in the kitchen, surrounded by eight or ten children, haven't you?' He looked back over his shoulder at Tish, one eyebrow raised.

'If I thought you really believed that, your rating would immediately go to zero,' Tish said, making a terrible face at him.

'And what makes you so sure I don't?' Nicholas asked. He leaned towards Tish and looked into her eyes searchingly as he put the plates down on the table. 'What makes you think you know so much about me?'

'I *know* that I know,' Tish corrected him. 'I know,' she said seriously, 'that you are a man of warmth and passion, of great devotion and concern for others, a man of courage.'

Nicholas's face darkened instantly. 'Courage?' he said scathingly.

Tish would not let him deny it. 'Yes, courage,' she repeated. 'You've had the courage to set your own, very difficult terms of atonement for something you believe you did wrong, and stick to them for a very long time. Not many people could do that.'

'Believe I did! Tish...'

'Enough!' Tish said, getting to her feet with one hand raised, signalling a halt. 'Let's not argue about it now. It only upsets my stomach to argue before a meal. We'll talk about it later.' She watched as Nicholas's dark frown slowly changed to allow a twinkle of amusement to return to the clear blue of his eyes.

'Sometimes I think you're a very bossy woman,' he said, handing her the silverware and napkins. 'I'm not sure I like that.'

'See?' Tish replied. 'I told you you might be jumping the gun with your proposal.'

They continued to banter light-heartedly throughout the meal, which Nicholas ate with a gusto that made Tish doubly glad she had brought it to him.

'The best turkey I ever ate,' he declared, patting his midsection and smiling at Tish. 'I guess I can't make you cook, after all. You'd have me fatter than a pig in no time.'

'I think you're just a good eater,' Tish replied. 'The only better one I've seen is my cat, Rocky.'

'Mmm, yes. I saw your cat that night I took you home.' Nicholas's expression was suddenly more guarded. 'It occurred to me that you specialise in taking in cripples.'

'You would think that,' Tish said, picking up a carrot stick and pointing at him with it. 'What you should have thought was that I was a person more interested in character than physical details. Rocky knows that. Why don't you?'

Nicholas shrugged. 'Maybe your cat's smarter than I am.' He looked at his watch. 'It's time to feed the horses. Let's save the dessert until later.'

'Good idea,' Tish agreed. 'Can I help?'

'Come along,' Nicholas said, giving her an amused smile. 'I doubt I could stop you anyway.'

'I do believe you're catching on,' Tish replied.

Tish put on her almost dry parka and boots, and Nicholas got into a heavy coverall and stocking cap. He led the way into the stables, where a huge space heater at either end roared away, managing to keep the worst of the chill from the air.

'I'm going to completely rebuild the stables next summer,' Nicholas said, raising his voice as they passed one of the propane heaters, 'and install a quieter heating system. These do the job all right, but the noise drives me crazy.'

'I don't blame you,' Tish shouted back. She followed Nicholas as he distributed hay to the horses, then went back to give each horse its own special ration of oats and other supplements.

'Some people have this all automated,' Nicholas told her, 'but I don't want to do that. I like to be able to talk to each horse and be sure he's doing all right.'

'Do they ever talk back?' Tish asked teasingly.

'In their own way,' Nicholas said, smiling.

Titan seemed to recognise Tish, and Nicholas let her feed him a special treat of some small pieces of fresh apple.

'He's so beautiful,' Tish said, sighing happily as the big horse nuzzled her hand, begging for more. She looked around at the big building, the stalls full of contented horses. Even with the storm roaring outside, it seemed so cosy. She took a deep breath and looked up at Nicholas, who was standing close beside her, his expression unreadable as he watched her. 'I like it here. I love the way it smells.'

Nicholas suddenly put his arm around Tish and pulled her close. 'You seem to belong here,' he said huskily.

Tish leaned against him, her head coming barely above his armpit. She did feel as if she belonged here, especially in the protection of Nicholas's arms. She looked up, her eyes meeting his with an impact that left her breathless. It was as if the guard he had put up had disappeared, leaving a clear view into his turbulent heart. Tish stared, fascinated by the depths she saw revealed, her own heart beating ever faster. The corners of Nicholas's mouth curved into a gentle smile.

'You're so tiny,' he said. He carefully pushed Tish's fur-trimmed hood back and ruffled her soft curls, then touched the tip of her small nose with his finger before caressing her cheek. 'If anything had happened to you out in that storm, I couldn't have stood it,' he said. 'It would have been my fault for having told you to stay away, when I think I knew all along that you wouldn't, especially after that note you sent back to me.'

'Nicholas Morgan, you are an idiot!' Tish cried, throwing her arms around him and hugging him as tightly as she could, her face buried against his chest. 'You aren't responsible for the fact that I'm a stubborn nitwit!' She looked up at him again, scowling. 'Will you please stop trying to carry the weight of the whole world around on your shoulders?'

'Is that what I'm doing?' Nicholas smiled wryly. 'Perhaps you're right.' He fondled Tish's cheek again, his eyes drifting slowly over her face, seeming to return several times to her lips.

Tish watched, holding her breath. She wanted him to kiss her, her entire body reacting with preliminary tingles to the thought. Instead, he shook his head.

'I hadn't better,' he said soberly, as if he knew what Tish was thinking. 'Given that you're destined to spend the night, we had better behave with circumspection now, or things might get out of hand.' All the while his head was bending closer and closer. He stopped, his mouth only inches from Tish's. Impulsively, she stood on tiptoe and flung her arms around his neck, bridging the final distance.

The reaction had been electric before. This time it created sheer pandemonium, sending Tish into a state of weightless flight that seemed to cancel all of the laws of gravity. The only thing constant was the strong embrace that gathered her in so tightly that she felt she had become part of the man who held her. Even in their wintry clothing there was communication that stripped away everything but the core of longing. Nicholas's mouth was less tentative this time, more demanding, his tongue invading, his mouth moving from side to side, as if he were drinking his fill with abandon. Then his lips left Tish's mouth, to course around her face, to nestle behind her ear where he whispered her name, over and over, like a song. While he did so, Tish stroked his hair, letting her fingers slide through the crisp, coppery silk, her eyes dreamily half closed. The lights of the stable seemed to flicker like fireflies dancing in the summer air. Things, she thought, were already out of hand, but she did not care. She startled, as if awakened from a dream, when Nicholas suddenly chuckled and raised his head.

'For a minute I thought those flickering lights were from us,' he said, 'but I think the power's about to go out. It usually does in a storm like this.'

'Then what do you do?' Tish asked.

Nicholas shrugged. 'Usually I start our emergency generator, but it's in another building and it would be foolhardy to try to get to it now. So we'll just throw some more wood on the fire, light some oil lamps, and wait for it to come back, which probably won't happen until the storm subsides and the repair crews can get out.'

'What a horrible fate, marooned here with you,' Tish said, sighing and leaning her cheek against Nicholas's chest.

'Tish,' Nicholas said, a stern note in his voice, 'unless you want us to make love later, you'd better back off. And unless you've decided to marry me, I'd rather we didn't.'

At those words, Tish stiffened and pulled back. She definitely did not want Nicholas to think she was promiscuous, and from her abandoned response to him he might get the wrong impression. With the uncompromising standards he set for himself, she was sure he would not like a woman who was.

'I'd prefer that, too,' she said. 'You see, I've never done that before. I've been waiting, but it hasn't been difficult at all ... until now.'

'Oh, Tish.' Nicholas held Tish tightly again for a moment and then released her. 'That was the most wonderful thing you could have said to me. Uh-oh. There they go.' The stables were suddenly plunged into darkness. 'Come on, let's go back to my room. I think I have space for some of that pie now.'

Nicholas was so buoyantly light-hearted while they ate their mince pie and then cleared the table together that

Tish felt that their relationship had suddenly reached another level. Could it be, she wondered, that he had never before had a woman tell him that she wanted him? Maybe thought that no woman ever would? It seemed quite possible, given the strength of his conviction that his scars made him ugly, but Tish was sure that she was not the only woman on earth who could see past those scars to the remarkable man behind them.

After the housekeeping chores were done, Tish curled up at one end of the sofa and Nicholas sprawled at the other. They asked each other inconsequential questions about what each of them had done before they really met each other, and found that they shared many memories, since both Tish and Nicholas had frequently been at the Greers' house.

'I'm afraid I never paid much attention to you and Mavis,' Nicholas said, his sense of mischief still prevailing. 'I was more interested in girls with shapes.' He traced a sexy outline in the air with his hands.

'And all I noticed about you was that you and Hal and Mike O'Hara seemed to think that Mavis and I were just something to step over when you came on to the front porch,' Tish countered. 'I didn't like any of you very much.' She was immediately sorry that she had mentioned Mike O'Hara's name, for Nicholas's face suddenly turned sad and withdrawn.

'Damn,' he said, leaning forward and burying his face in his hands. 'You'd made me forget for a while, for the first time in years.'

'Oh, Nicholas.' Tish edged down the length of the sofa and put her arm around his shoulders. She had wanted to hear Nicholas's own story about the tragedy, but not at the expense of his happy mood. 'I'm sorry,' she said. 'That was so thoughtless of me.'

Nicholas shook his head without lifting it. 'That's all right,' he said bitterly. 'It was bound to come between us sooner or later.'

'Come between us? Why?' Tish asked, backing away again as Nicholas impatiently removed her arm from his shoulders.

'Because,' Nicholas snapped, scowling at her, 'you can't spend the rest of your life trying to skirt the subject in order to keep me in a good humour, and it's not something I'm likely to get over.' He got to his feet and strode over to the window, staring out into the blackness. With a quick, powerful motion he pounded his fist against the wall. 'Damn it!' he swore. 'Damn it to hell! If only I could remember!'

Tish, who had been silently cursing her own lack of tact, was instantly alert. 'Remember?' she said softly, hoping that Nicholas would go on. 'What don't you remember?'

'Anything,' Nicholas replied. 'Anything about what happened.' He turned swiftly back toward Tish. 'Oh, it's not what you're thinking. I'm not repressing it. It simply isn't there.'

'I don't understand,' Tish said, shrugging helplessly.

Nicholas returned to sit beside her, his face tortured and intense. 'It's what they call retrograde amnesia,' he said. 'It can happen in the case of a severe head injury, such as I had. It seems that the trauma prevents what is known as memory consolidation from occurring. It's nothing mysterious, it's a neuro-chemical process that occurs when memories are put into long-term storage. It can be demonstrated quite nicely with rats. Give them a mild electrical shock, and they don't remember things that they recently learned. With humans, it can extend back for several days before the trauma. At first it did for me, but gradually some things came back. Now, it's like a wall comes down the day before the battle. I remember absolutely nothing between then and the time I came out of my coma in the hospital in Hawaii two months later. I keep hoping I'll remember, but...' he shrugged '...realistically, there isn't much hope. The only thing is that whenever I've talked to experts on the phenomenon, they always conclude with the statement that, of course, there are many things about human memory that are not well understood.'

'Then how do you know what happened?' Tish asked. 'Who told you?' Then a realisation suddenly dawned. 'Was it Mike O'Hara?'

'Yes,' Nicholas replied, his face contorted with pain. 'He was there. He saw it all.'

Tish stared at him, her own heart aching at the terrible pain in Nicholas's expression. What a cruel twist of fate that his good friend would have been the one to tell him. 'Wasn't it a little unusual,' she asked, 'to have both Mike and his brother in your platoon?'

Nicholas nodded. 'Just the luck of the draw,' he said wryly. 'For a while,' he went on, his voice low and husky, 'we thought it was great. After all, Mike and I had been buddies in high school, and Kevin ran around with us a lot too. I was their lieutenant, Mike was my platoon sergeant, and Kevin was just a private, but we thought of ourselves as a kind of three musketeers who could take on anything. And, for quite a while, we did. Mike and Kevin were the kind who got into a lot of the more unpleasant things that Vietnam had to offer, but they were both good soldiers. They never let me down. And then I...' His voice cracked, and he fell silent.

'When did Mike tell you?' Tish asked. There was something that she could not quite put her finger on, something that did not feel right to her. When Nicholas did not reply, she added, 'Please tell me, Nicholas. I need to know.'

Nicholas searched Tish's face with his haunted eyes for several minutes, as if looking for a reason to tell her. At last he nodded. 'Right after I'd been transferred back to the States. I was waiting for some reconstructive surgery. I found out he was at the same hospital, getting some work done on his leg, so I looked him up. At first he was so angry, so incoherent, that I could scarcely make out what he was saying. Then, when he found out that all I knew was that he was the only survivor, he told me the whole miserable story in exquisite detail. I had panicked when some incoming fire came from an unexpected direction and countermanded orders to go towards the Mekong River. We ran into an ambush...if you call being overrun by a couple of hundred Vietcong an ambush.' He looked at Tish and made a wry grimace. 'After hearing that, I decided not to have anything done to repair my face. I didn't feel I deserved to be alive, let alone look as if nothing had happened to me. And somehow...not remembering makes it doubly bad, as if I not only failed my men, but have abandoned them for ever.'

'Oh, Nicholas,' Tish breathed, her heart aching for him, but a strange uneasiness in her mind. She studied his tortured face thoughtfully, her eyes narrowed. He had accepted Mike O'Hara's story unquestioningly. He trusted Mike, his old friend. But what if Mike were not, for some reason, telling the truth? She carefully turned over in her mind the idea of suggesting to Nicholas that he might not have been, in the end discarding it, at least for the time being. He would probably be angry, thinking she was simply being unrealistic because she didn't want to believe him a coward. She would have to have something more substantial than her growing feeling of doubt to suggest before she presented that notion to Nicholas. Meanwhile, she would tuck it away in that corner of her mind with Charlie's glowing commendation until the time was right. That time, she knew with the utmost certainty, would eventually come.

Tish laid her hand on Nicholas's cheek, delicately tracing the scars with one finger.

'Does it hurt at all?' she asked.

Nicholas shook his head slightly, his eyes watching Tish intently.

She covered the scars with her hand, then removed it.

'It doesn't make much difference to what I see,' she said.

'Damn it, Tish, don't you understand what I've been saying?' Nicholas's voice was harsh, his hands, as he caught Tish's hands between them, exerting a painful pressure. 'Don't you understand?' he repeated. 'I can't ever forget. I can't ever be the kind of a man you'd want ...'

'Nicholas Morgan, you stop that!' Tish cried. 'I do understand. But I also think that something happened that you can't undo by withdrawing from life. Go on with your life. Make good things happen for the people who are still here, as you did for Peggy Willson. Of course you'll always remember, but not all of the time. There are other things that are important to think about, too. Your horses. The winery. Maybe even ... me.'

Nicholas looked down, caressing the small bones of Tish's hands with his large, blunt-edged fingers. He sighed heavily.

'I've tried to tell myself all that many times,' he said, 'but without much success. But then, I've never had anyone to help me before. Perhaps it can work if you'll help.' He looked up at Tish, searching her face carefully. 'Are you sure you can put up with a moody so-and-so like me long enough to find out?'

Tish smiled. 'If you can put up with a stubborn, ill-tempered woman who won't take no for an answer.' She caught her breath, her heart flooding with happiness at the radiant smile Nicholas gave her then. She had got through to him, had heard his story, and he was happy again. She trembled, barely able to control herself, as Nicholas slowly raised her hands and laid his cheek against them, then kissed each hand softly before he lowered them and smiled once again.

'Nicholas Morgan,' Tish said, her eyes misted and her voice husky, 'I do believe you're a very romantic man.'

'I've always thought I might be if I ever had the chance,' he replied. 'The question now is how to repress all of those impulses, since we're going to be sharing the same bed tonight.'

CHAPTER SIX

'Oh, my!' Tish's eyes flew wide open.

A glint more devilish than any she had yet seen lighted Nicholas's eyes.

'Why, Miss Holmsworth,' he said, 'what big eyes you have. And very green and beautiful, if I may say so.'

Tish made a face. 'Not now, you may not.' She patted the sofa. 'I suppose this is the bed? Couldn't I sleep on the floor?'

'Good lord, no! The floor isn't well insulated. It would be like ice, and I haven't anything to put down for you to sleep on. Don't look so worried. We've already agreed there's to be no pre-engagement hanky-panky. This is still pre-engagement, isn't it?'

'You know it is,' Tish grumbled. 'Why do you keep asking me every few minutes?'

Nicholas's face sobered. 'I'm sorry if it annoys you. It's only to help me remember that this isn't a dream. I never imagined anyone as exquisite as you could even consider me as a husband, and in my dreams I would simply have held out my hand to you the night of the rock concert and said, ''come and be mine'' and you would have said yes, just like in a fairy-tale. And, of course, when you kissed me I would have become a handsome prince for you.'

Tish gave him a reproving look. 'I think you're a handsome enough prince for any woman already, but somehow I find it hard to believe that you fell head over heels for me that night, green hair and all.'

Nicholas nodded. 'But I did. Green hair and all.' His eyes twinkled. 'I liked the way it matched your eyes. Come on, get up and I'll fix the bed.'

Tish stood up, watching as Nicholas removed the cushions and flipped open the couch. Since he had brought up the rock concert, perhaps it was safe to ask why he had gone.

'Why did you go to that concert? To find out if seeing Mike again might bring back some more of your memory?' she asked.

''I was wondering when you'd ask that,' Nicholas said, bringing a pile of bedding from a chest in the corner of the room. 'Maybe subconsciously a little hope I might remember something. Mostly morbid curiosity. I wondered if success had changed old Mike any over the years. Except for the weird haircut, he didn't look much different.' He looked up at Tish and grinned. 'But maybe it was fate, since I met you there.'

'Maybe,' Tish agreed. 'From the conversation at the party, I gathered he hadn't changed much. He's been married three times, which didn't seem to surprise anyone.' She helped Nicholas shake out a huge down quilt and place it over the flannel sheets. The bed looked so comfortable that suddenly she felt very sleepy. 'I guess I'll have to sleep in my clothes,' she said, yawning. 'I didn't plan on staying overnight.'

'That would be awfully uncomfortable,' Nicholas said, frowning thoughtfully. 'Let me see what I can find for you.' He rummaged in the cedar chest again, returning with a set of long winter underwear. 'Try this,' he said, handing it to Tish. 'You can change in the bathroom. I'll undress out here.'

'What are you going to wear?' she asked warily.

The devilry reappeared in Nicholas's eyes.

'Nothing,' he replied.

'Nicholas Morgan, you will too wear something!' Tish glared at him, her hands on her hips. 'I'll sit up all night if you don't.'

Nicholas chuckled. 'I was planning to leave on my long johns,' he said. 'We'll be a matching set.'

Tish shook her head at him and retreated to the bathroom, clutching the outfit Nicholas had given her. This was going to be quite an experiment, trying to sleep with him and keep her virtue intact. If the citizens of Laketown could see her now, they would never believe it. She had always been considered such a good girl, almost goody-goody, a reputation which had enabled her to get away with some real mischief now and then. Even Larry didn't believe at first that she had...

'Oh, good lord,' Tish said aloud, clapping her hand over her mouth in horror. If Larry ever found out that she had been stranded at Nicholas Morgan's stables overnight he would think the worst no matter what she said. Thank God, he was out of town. But if word got around, he would be both terribly angry and hurt. She did not want to marry him, but she didn't want to rub salt in his wounds, either. She had several times refused to go away with him for a weekend, even though he assured her they would have separate rooms. Mavis and Titus were the only ones who knew where she was. Mavis was sworn to secrecy, and Titus was the soul of discretion. If she had got home during the day there would have been no problem, but by the time she got back to town there would be a lot of people wondering where she had been. She was going to have to hope that no one saw her leave, when she finally did, and invent a real whopper for an explanation.

Her clothing change made, Tish returned to the main room to find Nicholas already in bed.

'Which side do you want?' he asked.

Tish shrugged, trying not to look at him, so huge and masculine in the rather small bed. 'I don't know. I never had to make that decision before.'

'Neither did I.' Nicholas raised himself up and looked around. 'I'll take the side nearest the stove,' he said. 'I may have to get up and throw some more wood on the fire during the night.' He moved over and then flipped the covers back for Tish. 'You look adorable in that outfit,' he said.

His compliment only added to Tish's nervousness. 'I look like the abominable snowman,' she said, looking down at the soft, white undergarments which, being sized for Nicholas, covered her small frame more like a tent than anything she could think of. She sat gingerly on the edge of the bed and looked over her shoulder apprehensively at Nicholas.

'I was just thinking,' she said, 'that if word gets out where I spent the night, my reputation will be ruined.'

Nicholas's expression immediately darkened. 'I suppose that wouldn't do any woman's reputation any good,' he said, his voice tinged with ice. 'I warned you about that, didn't I?'

'Oh, Nicholas, I didn't mean it that way!' Tish cried, getting under the covers and turning to face him, her heart sinking at the veil of cold withdrawal she saw in his eyes.

'Just go to sleep,' he said. He turned his back on her, then reached to turn out the lamp.

'Oh, God, I'm so stupid!' Tish said into the darkness, tears welling in her eyes. She got no argument, no reply at all. For several minutes she lay there, feeling sick with

misery. In one statement she had undone all of the good
from the day. If only Nicholas weren't so quick to jump
to the wrong conclusions. But then, it was all so new to
him, having someone who really cared about him. She
wasn't sure whether to call it love just yet, but it was
very close. She had cared about what Larry thought,
too, but not with the same wrenching intensity, as if every
emotion he felt was what she felt, too. Now Nicholas
was unhappy and she was miserable. She would never
be able to sleep a wink. They simply had to talk this
out. She had heard it said that, in good marriages, a
couple never went to sleep without resolving an argument. Well, although they weren't even engaged yet,
it was a good time to start following that rule. If they
couldn't, prospects for a future together were not very
bright.

'Nicholas?' Tish said softly. When there was again no
reply, she thumped on his back. 'Nicholas,' she said more
firmly, 'talk to me.' She told him of the rule she had
heard. 'I think we'd better start following it right now,'
she added. 'With my temper and your moodiness, we'd
be in the divorce court in six months after we married
if we don't.'

Nicholas made a growling sound, but he turned over
and faced Tish again.

'All right,' he said, 'explain what you meant, if I'm
wrong.'

Tish paused. She did not want to bring Larry Johnson
into the picture, especially not now. She would rather
deal with him and get him firmly out of the picture before
she even mentioned him to Nicholas. She would have to
keep her explanation more general.

'I think what you should know,' she said slowly, 'is
that my reputation in Laketown is as a regular Miss

Goody Two-Shoes. Since you may not have realised that, I can understand your reaction, but maybe it will help you to understand mine, too. As the editor of the newspaper, I'm a lot more visible than most people. People would be shocked to find out I'd spent the night with any man, and it's no good to deny anything happened, because the more you deny some things, the worse they get. Of course, given the blizzard, it's a little different, but I can't very well say I was on my way to somewhere else, because no one else I know lives on this road. And yes, because it's you people will say, ''What on earth was she doing, going there in that storm? She must have known she'd have to spend the night. Can she really be sleeping with Nicholas Morgan?'' They don't know you as I do, or all of the single girls in town would be here, and I'd have to stand in line. So, you're right, I will have to contend with that, but I don't mind as long as you're not angry with me. That's something I just can't stand. It takes all the joy out of life for me when you are.'

Nicholas sighed. 'I'm not angry with you, Tish. I don't want you to be hurt because of me, and you will be.'

'That's my choice, Nicholas,' Tish said firmly, 'not yours. You can hurt me far more than anyone else can. The rest will pass.'

For a long time Nicholas was silent. In the dim, flickering light from the wood stove, Tish watched his face intently. He seemed to be wrestling with some deep problem, his expression changing from thoughtful to worried several times. At last he spoke, his voice deep with emotion.

'I don't know if I ought to tell you this, Tish,' he said. 'I don't want to put any pressure on you by doing so, but it's the only way I know how to explain what I feel. You see, I love you. I love you so much that the thought of anyone hurting you is almost unbearable. I want to protect you from everything that might hurt you, but…' he smiled, reaching out to touch Tish's cheek with his hand, 'I guess I can't. And, God knows, I don't want to be the one to hurt you.'

'Oh, Nicholas!' Tish covered the short distance between them with one movement, and buried her face in the curve of his shoulder, her arms going around him to hold him tight. She held perfectly still, listening to the fast, strong beating of his heart, her own heart keeping joyful time. She was tempted to tell him that she loved him, too, but was not quite ready to make that leap. Nor did she want him to think that he had pried the confession from her. Quite soon, she thought, if things kept going as they were, she would be ready to tell him.

'Tish?' Nicholas said softly.

'Hmm?' she queried back from her cosy nest.

'If you hold very still, this may work out all right.'

Tish smiled to herself. There was such a soft, warm edge to Nicholas's deep voice when his natural good humour took over. It was beginning to happen more and more frequently.

'I'll be like a statue,' she promised. She could feel Nicholas kiss the top of her head.

'Tish?' he said again, his voice whimsical. 'Do you really think all the single girls might stand in line to be here?'

Tish chuckled. 'Goodnight, Nicholas,' she said.

'Goodnight, Tish,' he replied.

It was daylight when Tish next opened her eyes, to find Nicholas watching her. For a moment she was so dazzled by the depth of emotion she saw there that she could not speak, and Nicholas did not seem inclined to say anything, his warm smile speaking for him.

'Good morning,' she said at last. 'Did you sleep well?'

'Not very,' he replied, 'but I must confess it was the most pleasant night I've ever spent. I think I could look at you for ever.'

Tish felt a lump form in her throat.

'You say the sweetest, most romantic things,' she said huskily. She leaned up and gave him a quick kiss on the lips, then rolled away and sat up. 'However,' she said, giving him a meaningful look, 'I'm afraid that with both of us awake, just looking at each other might not be enough.' She got up and padded over to the window. 'The snow has stopped and the wind's died down,' she said, 'and it looks as if the sun is trying to peep through.'

Nicholas came to stand beside her. 'So it is,' he said with a sigh. 'I was hoping to have you trapped for another day or two. Now I'll have to get out my big tractor with the snow-blade and clear the drive so the staff can get in. Shall we have some breakfast and then get at it?'

'All right,' Tish agreed, also sighing. 'I guess it's back to the real world.'

They breakfasted quickly and almost silently, frequently exchanging little smiles that said more than any words could do. It was, Tish thought, as if a whole new world had dawned for both of them since the day before. They put on their warm clothing and went out into the vast whiteness of the snow-blanketed land.

'It sounds as if the county snow-crew is almost to the gate,' Nicholas said, holding still and listening intently. 'Hey, stop that!' as Tish tossed a snowball at him. He immediately scooped up some snow and tossed one back. A mêlée ensued with snowballs flying, and ended with

Tish running, squealing loudly, as Nicholas pursued her
with a large handful of snow, bent on stuffing it down
her neck.

'Help!' she cried, plunging headlong into a drift.

'Got you!' Nicholas responded, tumbling in after her.
Instead of chilling her with the threatened snow, he
grabbed her and kissed her thoroughly. 'I hope that was
punishment enough,' he said, releasing her at last and
pulling her to her feet.

'I've never suffered so much,' she replied, laughing.
'Do it again.'

'Oh, no. I've got work to do,' Nicholas answered, his
own laugh as happy as a young boy's.

Tish made a face at him, then turned her head,
frowning. 'It sounds as if they're very close with the
snowploughs,' she said.

'Yes, it does,' Nicholas agreed. 'I can't imagine...maybe Titus talked them into ploughing out the
front drive. Come on.' He held out his hand to Tish,
and together they made their way from the stables to
the mansion, rounding the corner just in time to see the
plough come to a halt behind Tish's car.

'How nice...' she began, then stopped, a sick knot
tightening her stomach like a physical blow. Larry
Johnson, his face contorted with rage, was emerging
from the snowplough vehicle. He leaped to the ground
and advanced on them, his burning eyes fixed on
Nicholas's face.

'You ugly so-and-so,' he snarled. 'You lousy, rotten...'

'Larry!' Tish cried. 'Stop that!'

'Shut up, Tish,' Larry said, without looking at her.
'You aren't going to get away with this,' he went on,
leering menacingly at Nicholas. 'I'm not going to let you
steal Tish from me, just because she has a heart as soft

as butter. She was all set to marry me until she started to feel sorry for you, but she'll get over it if you just stay the hell out of the picture.'

Tish watched in horror as Nicholas's face, at first only startled, hardened, his eyes turning into bleak pools of icy contempt.

'Gladly,' he replied, turning and walking rapidly away.

'Nicholas, wait!' Tish cried, running after him and catching him by the arm. 'I never...'

'Let go of me,' Nicholas growled, shaking her loose. He stopped and looked down at her, no emotion at all now showing on the bitter landscape of his scarred face. 'Go back to town,' he said, 'and stay there, where you belong.'

CHAPTER SEVEN

WATCHING Nicholas walk away, Tish felt as if her heart was actually breaking. Never had she felt more like crying her eyes out, but never had she been more determined not to shed a single tear. When she was through with Larry Johnson, he was going to wish he had never been born! She turned and walked slowly towards him, trying to compose herself enough to be coherent.

'Miserable coward didn't have much to say for himself, did he?' Larry commented when she drew near. 'He didn't harm you, did he?'

Tish longed to slap his smooth, smug face, but she restrained herself. 'No, of course not,' she replied in silky tones. 'Tell me, Larry, how did you know I was here? And why are you here? I thought you went to see your parents.'

'When it started to snow, I decided not to go,' he replied. 'I didn't want to get stuck in Rochester. We get along fine for the first twenty-four hours, but after that it's not much fun.'

'Oh,' Tish said, feigning surprise. 'I didn't know that.' But I might have guessed, she added to herself. A man whose strongest emotions were aroused by jealousy, rather than love, doubtless had some other problems, too. Too bad she hadn't thought about that before.

'Mavis told me where you'd gone,' Larry went on. 'At first she said she didn't know, but after I'd called everyone else I could think of I tried her again. She said then you'd gone to see some friends in the country. I convinced her you might be trapped in your car, and then she confessed.' He looked at Tish with a worried frown. 'You could have been, you know.'

Tish smiled sweetly. 'But I wasn't, was I?'

'No, but I stayed awake all night, not knowing whether I was more worried about that or about your spending the night with Nicholas Morgan. I was the one who got the snow plough to come out this way first thing and made them let me ride along with them.'

'How nice,' Tish said. She watched as the snow plough turned and went back out the drive. That certainly sealed the fact that everyone in Laketown would know where she had been, but she no longer cared. 'Come on,' she said to Larry. 'I'll drive you home. You must be exhausted from your all-night vigil.'

Larry gave her a strange look, but got silently into her car. 'I must say,' he said when he had seated himself and Tish had started the car, 'that you're taking this very well. I probably shouldn't have let go at Morgan like that, but when I saw him with you...'

'I know,' Tish said, gritting her teeth to keep from saying more. 'We'll talk about it when we get back to town.' She drove as fast as possible on the still snowy road, trying not to listen as Larry babbled on about how she should have more concern for her reputation, more concern about his feelings. At last she reached the driveway of Larry's house and turned in.

'Come on in and have some coffee,' Larry said, reaching for the door-handle.

'No, Larry,' Tish said very softly. 'Just stay here. I have some things to say to you, and then you can go and have coffee all by yourself.'

Larry sat back and looked questioningly at Tish. 'What do you mean? Do you have to get to work already?'

A wave of exasperation swept through Tish and her control suddenly snapped.

'No!' she shouted. 'I mean it is time you got it through your head that I am not going to marry you, ever! In fact, after your disgusting display this morning, I wouldn't marry you if you were the last man on earth! You and your pompous self-righteousness! You aren't one-tenth the man that Nicholas Morgan is! I don't pity him, I pity you! I know you care about me, in your own strange, self-centred way. I didn't want to hurt you. I even thought for a while that I ought to consider marrying you; you made it all sound so logical. But marriage isn't something I care to go into like an accountant figuring a balance sheet. It may work for you, but it could never work for me. Now get out of my car, forget me, and find yourself some nice little woman who can accept your fits of jealousy as a substitute for passion!'

Larry's face had become quite pale during Tish's discourse, his eyes fixed in an unbelieving stare. He licked his lips nervously.

'Now, Tish...' he began.

Tish wished fervently that she were big enough to shake some sense into the man. As it was, all she could do was to level one last blast and then order him from her car.

'Don't say "now, Tish" to me!' she yelled, leaning towards him. 'I have meant every word that I said. I will not marry you. I do not want to see you again. Ever! And if you persist in harassing me I will get an injunction preventing you from coming within ten miles of me!'

'You can't do that,' Larry said, his lip now curling in contempt. 'You're crazy. You've gone clear off your rocker over that Morgan guy. What do you plan to do, marry him?' He spat out the last words in disgust.

Tish almost shot back that she certainly did, but stopped herself. She was not quite ready to tell Nicholas that she would marry him, and it wasn't the sort of thing she should say just to shock Larry. Besides, God only knew whether she could ever repair the damage that Larry had done and get Nicholas back to asking her. Instead she waited until she had regained her self-control. There was no point, she decided, in continuing this conversation any longer.

'Wait and see,' she said. 'Now get out. I do have to get to work.'

Larry gave her another contemptuous look, then got out of the car. 'You'll be sorry,' he said, before slamming the door as hard as he could.

Not half as sorry, Tish thought bitterly, as she was that she hadn't got rid of Larry Johnson before. He had certainly shown his true colours this day! She heaved a tired sigh. It was only ten in the morning, she was already emotionally exhausted, and she had a newspaper to get out before she could go back and try to talk to Nicholas, who was doubtless going to have a perfectly awful day himself.

Fortunately, the newspaper went together quite smoothly. Jeff and several other of Tish's student assistants were on hand all day, thanks to the school holidays. The blizzard itself had generated a lot of news and some exceptional pictures, and there were the usual items about who visited whom for Thanksgiving dinner and which out-of-town guests couldn't make it because of the storm. Tish knew that the story of her venture had already spread when the mayor's wife, after reciting her own guest list, asked in hushed tones, 'You didn't actually spend Thanksgiving with Nicholas Morgan, did you?'

'Yes, I did, Mrs Braman,' Tish replied cheerfully.

'And . . . the night?'

Tish almost choked trying not to laugh at the woman's tactlessness. 'That's right,' she said. 'The roads were closed, remember?'

'Oh, yes. Of course. It must have been quite an . . . experience, staying in that place.'

'Quite,' Tish said, now growing irritated. 'Do you have some more news for me?' When the woman did not, Tish wished her a nice day and hung up. She knew the gossipy woman would spend the rest of the day on the telephone, spreading the story, no doubt embroidering it as she went. She would probably say she had *pried* the information out of Tish Holmsworth, that she hadn't really wanted to say very much about it, no wonder she was trying to hide it, and so on. 'I'll fix that,' Tish muttered. She inserted a piece of paper into her typewriter and quickly typed out her own news item:

> Tish Holmsworth took a surprise turkey dinner to Nicholas Morgan on Thanksgiving Day. As is his custom, Mr Morgan had given his staff the day off, and was spending the day at his small apartment at his stables. Both participants enjoyed the dinner very much, and were pleased that Ms Holmsworth's visit was prolonged when the snowstorm prevented her returning to town until the next morning.

'There!' Tish said, handing the item to Jeff. 'Add that to the local gossip column.'

Jeff took the item, read it, then grinned. 'Beating them to the punch, huh?'

'You've got it,' Tish replied. Her telephone rang and she grimaced. 'Most of them, anyway,' she said. 'Hello? Oh, hello, Mavis. A fine friend you turned out to be.'

'I'm sorry, Tish,' Mavis said, sounding hurt, 'but I was worried about you, too. Poor Larry was frantic. And he is again. What did you say to him? He just called and was absolutely incoherent. All I could make out was that I'm supposed to talk some sense into you before you do something stupid.'

Tish felt her temper begin to simmer again. 'Mavis,' she snapped, 'I am not the stupid one, he is. I can't talk about it now. I've got to go home and clean up when I'm through here in about an hour. Meet me there, will you?'

'Of course,' Mavis agreed. 'See you.'

Back at home, Tish simultaneously showered, changed, and talked to Mavis, who sat curled up on Tish's bed, a thoughtful frown beneath her blonde bangs as she heard Tish's story of her time with Nicholas, Larry's disastrous entrance, and the task she now had to reassure Nicholas that she was not about to marry Larry Johnson.

'What is wrong with Larry?' Tish asked, standing in her slip with her hands on her hips. 'Why does he persist? I've never told him either that I love him or that I'll marry him. Why won't he take no for an answer?'

Mavis shook her head. 'I'm sure I don't know. I guess some people are like that. Hal had a girl after him once that was. No matter what he said, she just kept coming back. He finally had to get an unlisted telephone number to keep her from bothering him at all hours of the night.'

'Oh, lord, I hope it doesn't come to that,' Tish said with a sigh. 'Well, if he bothers you again, try to get my message through, will you? Maybe if he hears it from enough people it will.'

She went to her wardrobe and found a soft green angora sweater and plaid skirt to put on, then brushed her curls until they shone.

'Do I look all right?' she asked, smoothing her skirt anxiously.

'Perfect,' Mavis replied. 'Does Nicholas appreciate your...physical virtues? Does he pay compliments?'

'Oh, yes,' Tish said. 'He says the sweetest things. And he has the dearest smile. I love to see him smile. I love his face, when he's happy. I don't notice his scars at all. It's as if they aren't even there.' She bit her lip. 'I wish you could have seen his face when that awful Larry...'

Suddenly all of the tears that Tish had felt like shedding that morning came streaming from her eyes. Mavis jumped up and put an arm around her, and led her to sit on the bed beside her.

'There, there, sweetie, it will be all right. Nicholas will understand, I know he will.'

'I—I hope so,' Tish sobbed.

Mavis hugged her friend and patted her shoulders. 'Come on, now, dry your tears so you'll look beautiful. You love Nicholas, don't you?'

Tish nodded. 'Yes. I love him very much.' She looked at Mavis mournfully. 'I can't bear it that people think he's a coward, and it hurts even worse that he believes it too, because...because I know he isn't. If I could only find Charlie...'

'Whoa, there,' Mavis said. 'Charlie? Charlie who?'

For the first time, Tish described her encounter with the man named Charlie, along with Nicholas's story of his amnesia for the entire period of the battle and the day before.

'After all, Charlie, whoever he is, had to have been there when Nicholas was wounded,' Tish concluded, 'and he might have an entirely different story to tell from Mike O'Hara's, but he obviously wasn't a regular member of Nicholas's platoon, nor a very close friend. Worst of all, I haven't the slightest idea where to begin looking for the man.'

'Whew!' Mavis breathed. 'That is a hard one, but I'll think about it and see if I get any bright ideas. You know...' she frowned thoughtfully, 'I'm not sure that Hal knows that Nicholas can't remember, and I don't think he's ever felt completely comfortable with Mike's story, either.'

'Oh? Why do you say that?' Tish questioned.

'He'd never told any of us. I'd never heard it before. I always assumed it was the scars that made Nicholas hide away. And you know how Hal acted at the party when Mike told it. He was furious.' Mavis frowned. 'I've never trusted Mike O'Hara, ever since he stole my ice-cream quarter when I was six years old. He told me he could make it disappear like magic. I thought he was going to do some kind of trick, but all he did was put it in his pocket and walk away.'

'Did he pull that on you, too? That stinker!' Tish exclaimed. She got up and peered into the mirror. 'I guess I'll have to do,' she said with a sigh. 'I can't take time now to figure out how to find a Charlie needle in the whole United States haystack. I have to go and beard a very fierce lion in his den. But one of these days, let's get together and brainstorm it a bit, shall we?'

'Definitely,' Mavis replied. She frowned thoughtfully. 'Why don't you see if Nicholas remembers someone named Charlie from Vietnam? Anyone at all?'

Tish nodded. 'I intend to. I may even tell him the whole story, I don't know. I'll have to play it by ear.' She put on her winter coat and picked up the copy of the day's *Laketown Herald*, in order to show Nicholas the item she had put in about them. If, that was, he would even talk to her. 'Wish me luck,' she said, as the two women went out the door together.

'I do,' Mavis replied, 'but don't worry, everything will work out. I know it will. And you and Nicholas have my blessing, if it helps any.'

'It helps a lot,' Tish replied.

She drove along the road to the Morgan estate, rehearsing over and over in her mind what she would say, with variations depending on Nicholas's response. When she got to the gates, Titus came out and stopped her.

'I'm afraid I can't let you in, Letitia,' he said, a mournful look on his kindly, lined face. 'I have strict orders.'

'Oh, Titus, don't do this to me,' Tish wailed, tears welling in her tired eyes. 'Nicholas won't be angry if you let me in, really he won't. I've got to talk to him. He got all the wrong ideas from Larry Johnson this morning. I'm not going to marry that idiot. I never was. I'm going to marry...' Tish suddenly realised that for the second time that day, she was about to say something more than a little hasty. Well, it was true. She knew it now. She did love Nicholas, and she did want to marry him. But there was a strong chance that Nicholas might not still want her, especially if she didn't get to talk to him.

Titus was bending toward her, his eyes wide with interest. The dear old man would never stand in the way of true love, she knew, and it might be her only chance to get past him. She swallowed. 'Nicholas,' she finished, in a low voice. 'If he'll still have me.'

'Well, well,' Titus said, a smile as wide as his wrinkled cheeks would permit lighting his face. 'Things have progressed, haven't they?'

'They were progressing,' Tish replied, heaving an extra loud sigh and wiping away her tears with a gloved hand. 'I hope I can straighten them out again.'

'So do I, Letitia,' Titus said, his smile fading into a pursed, tight line. 'Mr Morgan needs someone like you, after all he's been through. People have been very unfair to him. I'll let you in and phone ahead and tell Winchell to do the same. Don't mind him if he looks cross. He always does.'

'Thank you, Titus,' Tish said, heaving a sigh of relief this time. 'Don't tell anyone what I told you, will you? I'd look a terrible fool if things don't work out.'

'Of course I won't, Letitia,' Titus said, looking hurt at the very idea. Then he smiled again and winked. 'Good luck.'

The gates swung open, and Tish drove on through, bracing herself for her encounter with Winchell, the butler. Getting to see Nicholas Morgan was like running a gauntlet! And that was before her real trials began.

The butler opened the door before Tish could ring the bell, a look of stern disapproval on his face.

'Come in, Miss Holmsworth,' he said in a raspy voice. 'I told Mr Titus that Mr Morgan had already retired, but he said it was an emergency that you see him.'

'Yes, it is,' Tish confirmed as staunchly as she could, given that the cavernous foyer made her feel as large and brave as a mouse.

'Mr Morgan is in his suite on the second floor,' Winchell said. 'Come with me.' He led the way slowly up the stairs, and into a corridor as long and high-ceilinged as a grand old hotel, the walls dotted with pictures that Tish assumed were the Morgan ancestors. Winchell finally paused and knocked firmly on a door.

'What is it?' came the gruff reply.

'Don't say my name!' Tish whispered quickly, fearing the worst if Winchell announced her presence. 'Tell him you have an emergency.'

The old butler gave Tish a reproving look, but he followed her instructions. 'Winchell here, sir,' he answered. 'I have . . . a small emergency.'

There was the sound of heavy footsteps approaching the door, and then it was flung open. Nicholas stood there in a midnight-blue robe, a drink in one hand.

'What . . .' he began, then his eyes fell on Tish.

'Hello, Nicholas,' Tish said, her heart almost stopping at the cold misery she saw in his face. 'I'm the small emergency.'

Nicholas glared first at her, and then at Winchell, who quickly retreated.

'How in hell did you con everyone into letting you in?' he demanded. His lip curled in disgust. 'But then, you're very good at that sort of thing, aren't you?'

'No, I'm not!' Tish denied hotly. 'Not nearly as good as you are at jumping to the wrong conclusions.'

'Wrong?' Nicholas gave a short, dry laugh. 'After the way you convinced me you might actually give a damn about me, and then I find myself insulted by a man who apparently thought you were going to marry him? I'd say you have an almost psychopathic ability to make people believe whatever you want them to believe.'

Tish set her mouth in a tight line, trying to keep back the tears that were again trying to come. This was not going well at all, and if she didn't do something quickly, Nicholas would shut his door and all would be lost. She looked past Nicholas, who was leaning with one arm against the doorframe, into a huge sitting-room, complete with chairs and a sofa before a blazing fire in a marble fireplace. If she could get inside... With a sudden, quick movement she ducked under his arm and then turned to face him. 'You may as well shut the door and sit down,' she said, 'because I'm not going to leave until I've said my piece.'

Nicholas shook his head, his face drawn and tired. 'Get out, Tish,' he said in a lifeless voice. 'I've heard enough of your glib explanations to last me a lifetime.' He walked over to Tish, put his hand on her back, and started propelling her towards the door.

'No!' she cried, twisting away from him and running towards the sofa. She took off her coat and flung it down. 'You're going to listen to me right now. Then, if you still want me to go, I will.'

Nicholas shrugged and closed the door, but said nothing.

'This won't be very glib or very long. I'm too tired,' Tish said, clutching at the sofa back and trying to rally her trembling nerves for one last time. 'I am not in love with Larry Johnson, I never was, never told him I was. Never, ever, did I say I'd marry him. He kept trying and trying to convince me I should. I didn't give him a definite no for a long time because I did like him and I thought maybe I was being foolish and impractical. After all, I'm twenty-seven, and there aren't many eligible men

around, and my father approved of him. Then, when
he tried to get me to set a wedding date, I realised I
couldn't. I finally told him absolutely no, and then he
convinced himself it was because of you, not because I
really didn't want to. I stopped seeing him, I stopped
talking to him, but he still didn't give up. He pestered
Mavis yesterday until she told him where I'd gone, and
I guess he spent the night reconvincing himself that if it
weren't for you I'd marry him. Well, I won't, as I told
him all over again this morning. I even threatened him
with an injunction if he doesn't stop harassing me. And
that's the whole story, except...' Tish gulped down the
tears that were trying to come at the sight of Nicholas's
still grim expression. 'Except,' she said hoarsely, 'that
I'm so very sorry that you had to find out the way you
did this morning. I should have told you about him, I
guess, but I...'

Nicholas was still staring at Tish, his face blank of
emotion. Oh, God, she thought, he didn't believe me!
He doesn't care! A racking sob shook Tish's body, and
she bolted towards the door, blinded by tears. She was
fumbling for the doorknob, when a pair of strong arms
surrounded her and swept her up. Swiftly, Nicholas
carried her to the sofa by the fire and sat down with her
in his arms, then cradled her tenderly against his
shoulder. He stroked her back soothingly until her sobs
subsided.

'Can I say my piece now?' he asked, his voice suspiciously hoarse.

Tish nodded against his shoulder, afraid to look at
him yet, but longing to see the dark shadows lift from
the clear blue of his eyes.

'I'm sorry you didn't tell me sooner, too,' he said,
'but I can understand why you didn't. You were probably

afraid that if you mentioned another man in your life I'd be suspicious and unreasonable, and I probably would have. I'm not an easy man to get along with, as you've already found out. Perhaps you ought to give Larry Johnson another chance...'

'Good lord, no!' Tish cried, raising up and staring at Nicholas in horror. 'What was it you said to me yesterday? Something about not understanding anything you'd said? I couldn't possibly marry Larry. He has no passion, no real warmth. The only thing that gets him really aroused is jealousy, and I can't spend my life with someone like that!'

Nicholas shook his head, his brow still furrowed. 'No,' he said slowly, 'I wouldn't want you to.'

'I should hope not!' Tish raised one hand and smoothed the still deep lines of anxiety around Nicholas's eyes. She smiled gently. 'Why do you suppose I came here tonight?'

'I can't imagine,' Nicholas replied wryly, although the dark unhappiness was beginning to disappear from his face, some of the sparkle returning to the clear blue of his eyes.

'I came here,' Tish said, 'to see a man who is exciting and warm and loving and romantic and passionate about many things he cares about.' She traced the curve of Nicholas's lips with her finger. 'And,' she said, 'who has the most beautiful smile I've ever seen.' At that, Nicholas finally smiled, and Tish felt a surge of relief and happiness that made her own smile wide and joyous.

'Funny,' he said, 'but that's how I would describe you.' His smile faded again. 'I'd be more inclined to describe myself as a stupid idiot who doesn't deserve the good fortune of having you in his arms right now, but who is very glad that he does.'

'Oh, Nicholas,' Tish said, taking his face between her hands, 'you're not stupid at all, you're just not used to having someone love you. And I do, Nicholas. I love you with all my heart.'

Nicholas closed his eyes for a moment and then re-opened them, tears sparkling on his lashes, his expression a mixture of awakening joy and disbelief.

'Did I just hear what I think I heard?' he asked.

'I love you,' Tish repeated.

'Good lord,' he said, a smile of wonder dawning on his face, 'what did I do to suddenly become the luckiest man on earth?'

Tish smiled back, and then closed her own eyes, as Nicholas's arms enveloped her and his mouth sought hers in a kiss of such driving passion that her tiredness and sorrow vanished in a sweep of fire that ravaged every inch of her body and left her giddy with longing. Their mouths sought every taste, every angle, with an insatiable hunger, their bodies straining together, hands exploring frantically. Together they rolled from the sofa on to the thick carpet. Tish's sweater came off, and Nicholas worshipped at the soft curves of her breasts, his lips turning delight into a drenching desire.

'Oh, Tish,' he said hoarsely, raising his head to stare into her eyes, his own eyes almost black with wanting. 'I can't live without you any longer.'

'Are we engaged?' she whispered against his lips.

'Do you want to be?' he asked between delicious little kisses.

'Yes,' Tish replied. 'I do want to be.'

Nicholas drew back and looked at her soberly. 'You're sure, now? You aren't just saying that because we both want to make love? Because if we're engaged, that means we're going to be married before very long, and that means spending the rest of your life with me.'

'That, Nicholas Morgan,' Tish said, caressing his scarred cheek gently, 'is exactly what I thought it meant.'

CHAPTER EIGHT

NICHOLAS smiled radiantly. 'Then I suggest we move to a more comfortable place. I don't think this is the best spot for your first experience at making love.' He got to his knees and held his arms out to Tish. 'Let me carry you off to my bed, lovely princess,' he said.

'All right,' Tish said, feigning reluctance, but putting her arms around Nicholas's neck, 'but having our love-life start here would have made a rather exciting anecdote in my memoires.'

'I think you could still say that it did,' he replied, gathering Tish into his arms and smiling down at her. He stood and carried her into the adjoining room, a room so ornate and elegant that Tish gasped at the sight of it. Rococo cherubs bearing gilded harps decorated the edges of a ceiling of intricate plaster-work. A delicate floral silk lined the walls, and the bed...

'My mother's doing,' Nicholas said, chuckling as Tish stared wide-eyed at the huge bed, with its pale blue velvet headboard and creamy satin coverlet. 'She was a very romantic woman, and I've kept it the way she left it, dreaming that some day I would find the perfect woman to bring here myself.' He tumbled Tish on to the bed and leaned across her, brushing her lips with his own. 'And now I have,' he said softly.

'And I have found the perfect man,' Tish murmured. She slid her hands inside Nicholas's robe and pushed it from his shoulders, her fingers kneading the powerful muscles her action had revealed. In a quick movement,

Nicholas shrugged his robe off the rest of the way, groaning in pleasure as Tish then stroked his bare chest.

'Do you mind if I undress you the rest of the way before you drive me completely wild?' he asked, leaning back and trailing his fingertips from Tish's chin to her tummy.

Tish shivered in delight and shook her head. 'No, not at all,' she replied, feasting her eyes on the strong masculine body that now rose above her as Nicholas began to remove the rest of her clothing with deft, gentle hands. She had always thought she might feel uncomfortable when the time finally came to give herself to a man, but she had nothing but sensations of blissful happiness now. She wanted to be free to feel everything, to let her body touch and be touched by the man she loved. Moments later, she lay naked against the cool satin coverlet, the warmth of Nicholas's body stretched against hers.

'You feel so good to me,' he said, his eyes half closed, but communicating a deep, barely checked fire burning within that found an answering flame in Tish's heart. When he reached out to pull her closer, she burrowed against him eagerly, circling his broad back with her arm to help his quest. The strength and urgency of his desire invaded her mouth with a tongue that teased and tantalised and dominated her own. Their bodies moved and shifted together in an increasingly demanding rhythm, sending Tish into a soaring world of both insatiable hunger and the deepest satisfaction. To know this man she loved could want her so moved her beyond measure. To know that he could arouse her to heights she had never before imagined made her giddy with joy. Daringly, she flung her leg across Nicholas to tell him that she was ready to be his. Very gently he removed it.

'Let's not rush, now that we don't have to,' Nicholas murmured in Tish's ear. He raised his head. 'I'm trying to remind myself that this is only the first of many nights like this. I want to be sure it's perfect for you.'

'I don't think it could be any more perfect,' she replied. She pulled his head down to kiss him again, but he resisted, instead lowering his head to teach her what he meant with kisses that traced her body up and down with a shower of fiery delights, and caresses so soft that she imagined the angels on the ceiling had flown down to touch her with their gentle wings. 'Oh, Nicholas,' she moaned softly, her fingers kneading his shoulders. 'I want you so much.' She watched his dear face as he moved above her, his eyes alight with love. Then she heard the sound of a telephone ringing, and saw his smile turn instantly to a dark frown.

'What in the devil...' he exclaimed, pushing himself away from Tish and passing his hand across his eyes in a gesture of frustration.

'Don't answer it,' Tish said, reaching toward him.

Nicholas shook his head impatiently. 'I have to. It's some problem at the stables. Those are the only calls that come through to me at night.'

Tish sat up and hugged her knees, feeling suddenly cold and trembling. She watched with a worried frown as Nicholas crossed the room to a telephone on a small table by the windows.

'What is it?' he said without any preliminaries. Then he swore loudly. 'I'll be right there,' he snapped out in a harsh voice, then banged the receiver down. He glanced over at Tish. 'There was a small fire and some smoke,' he said at the same time as he began grabbing some clothing from an armoire and putting it on. 'They can't get Titan calmed down. God only knows how it happened, but when I find out...'

Tish jumped to her feet immediately. 'I'm coming with you,' she said, putting her own things back on as fast as her shaky fingers would permit.

'No, Tish,' Nicholas began, then he smiled wryly. 'I should know better than to tell you that, shouldn't I?' He came to her side, already dressed in a heavy sweatsuit and a parka. 'If I were any more frustrated, I could probably bite nails in half,' he said. 'Are you all right?'

'More or less,' Tish replied, with a grimace. 'Maybe next time we should go ahead and rush.' She got on her coat and followed Nicholas as he hurried down the stairs and through the back part of the lower floor, which included what she briefly noted must be a breakfast-room, a pantry, and a huge kitchen. The moonlight on the snow was so bright that there was no need for the flashlight which Nicholas had brought, and Tish saw with relief that there was no sign of smoke coming from the stables.

There was no smell of smoke inside the stables, either, only the sound of an agitated horse stomping and whinnying and a man cursing. The groom, Stanley, was standing outside Titan's stall wringing his hands.

'Stop it, Eben! Stop it, man!' he repeated over and over, only stopping himself when he saw Nicholas bearing down on him.

Nicholas wasted no time. He flung open the door to the stall, and grabbed an older man who was frantically beating at Titan and screaming, 'Down, boy. Down, you devil!'

The frightened horse was running back and forth, rearing up to beat his hooves against the walls, tossing his head, rolling his eyes and whinnying loudly. Nicholas collared the man and pushed him outside.

'Don't you move a muscle until I'm through here,' he snarled.

Tish watched for a moment as the man walked, head down, across the stables and stood leaning against another stall, breathing hard. Then she turned her attention back to Titan. In seconds, Nicholas had caught Titan's bridle with his hand, restraining his anxious movements, walking him around ever more slowly and talking to him gently. When the horse finally came to a halt, Nicholas stroked him and talked to him until at last, when he released him, he stood calmly, munching on a handful of some special treat which Nicholas had pulled from his pocket.

As the drama played out, Tish moved to stand next to Stanley, curious about what had precipitated the problem.

'What happened?' she asked in a low voice.

'Old Eben dropped his pipe in Titan's stall. It set a bit of straw on fire and frightened the horse. Eben got the fire out in a flash, but he got upset when Titan kept rearing, and he started hitting him. I couldn't get him out of there.'

'I wouldn't think the man would have a lighted pipe in here,' Tish said, frowning. 'Doesn't he know any better? Doesn't he know anything about handling horses?' It seemed very strange that Nicholas would keep someone around with no more sense than that.

Stanley shook his head sadly. 'Eben knows, for sure. He's worked for the Morgans for years, but he's not been himself lately. It's his wife, you see. They've been married for almost fifty years and she's dying of cancer. Eben's frantic with worry. And now he's probably lost his job.'

'Oh, my.' Tish looked across the stable at the elderly man, leaning dejectedly against the side of an empty stall. 'But surely, if he tells Mr Morgan...'

'He won't, ma'am. That's not a proper excuse.'

At that moment, Nicholas emerged from Titan's stall and made straight away for the older man. By the look of anger on his face, Tish could tell that Stanley's prediction of the man losing his job was doubtless correct. She turned and walked to the far end of the stables, but was still able to hear all too easily as Nicholas condemned the man for his errors, and terminated his employment in no uncertain terms. She looked up apprehensively when she heard Nicholas's footsteps approaching. As she had feared, he still looked furious.

'Damned old fool,' Nicholas growled. 'Could have burned down the stables.'

Tish nodded and thrust her hands into her pockets. It was, after all, Nicholas's business to deal with his employees. And, if the old man chose not to defend himself, it certainly wasn't up to her to do so. She followed Nicholas silently back into the snowy, moonlit night. Suddenly he stopped and confronted her.

'What's the matter, Tish? And don't tell me nothing is, because I can tell differently. I know you were listening. You think I was too hard on the old man, don't you? Well, you may as well get this straight right now. I'm in charge of running things around here, and I don't want you interfering.'

Tish bristled. 'I am not interfering! I haven't said a word, have I?'

'No, but you're sulking,' Nicholas replied. 'Johnson was certainly right about one thing. Your heart is as soft as butter. Which,' he added, smiling cajolingly, 'is all right, except when it comes to running a business.'

'I suppose you have to have one like granite to do that,' Tish retorted.

Nicholas scowled. 'Granite! For God's sake, Tish, do you have any idea how well I pay my people? How careful I am to see that they're well insured against accidents and injuries?'

'Which protects you even more than it does them,' she replied scathingly. At Nicholas's darkening frown, she felt suddenly contrite. 'Look, Nicholas,' she said, putting her hand on his arm, 'let's just forget it, shall we? You're right, I'm a softy. I've never been any good at firing people.' She looked at her watch, clearly visible in the bright moonlight. 'It's getting very late and I'm exhausted. Would you mind walking me around to my car? I have to be up early and get a newspaper out.'

'All right.' Nicholas sighed, then smiled wryly and put his arm around Tish as they walked along. 'It seems something or someone is always coming between us being together, doesn't it? Let's not put the wedding off for very long. I want you here, with me.'

At the sound of Nicholas's words, Tish felt a little warning bell go off somewhere in her mind. Did he think she planned to leave the newspaper as soon as they were married? She paused when they reached her car, and looked up at him.

'I'm not planning to quit the newspaper as soon as we're married,' she said. 'It belongs to my father, and I can't just drop it like a regular job. Besides, I love doing it.'

'Oh.' Nicholas looked disturbed, but he shrugged and gave Tish a little smile. 'We'll talk about that later,' he said. 'I just meant I wished you didn't have to go home now.'

'So do I,' Tish agreed. She put her arms around Nicholas's neck. 'We have a lot to talk about. Why don't you come to my house for dinner tomorrow night? I'm tired of fighting my way past the gates and the butler.'

'I'd like that,' Nicholas said.

He pulled Tish close, kissing her gently, but somehow she still felt too upset to respond, and when he raised his head and she pressed close against him for several minutes she still did not feel as warm and happy as before. Perhaps, she thought, she was just too tired from the events of the day. It had been more tumultuous than any she could remember.

But, as she drove home, she still felt unsure. Perhaps it had all happened too fast. She loved Nicholas, but they still had so many things to talk about, so many problems to resolve. She should probably have stayed and talked tonight and forgotten her need for sleep, but she had been half afraid that either she or Nicholas would get angry and start shouting or...she smiled wryly to herself...have started with one of those kisses that did ignite a fire and ended up back in bed, with nothing discussed at all. At the moment that sounded preferable to her cold, lonely bed, even if Rocky did cuddle up next to her and purr.

She turned down the quiet street that led to her house, started to turn into the driveway, and then stopped, all of her fatigue suddenly gone in a flash of anger. There, parked beside her door, was Larry Johnson's car, and the light was on in her kitchen! She had forgotten that she had given him a key so that he could feed Rocky when she had been away at the convention the previous summer. And he, the swine, had never returned it! Well, he could just give it back and get out of her house right now!

Tish parked in the street and hurried to her door, using her own key rather than knock and let Larry open the door as if he belonged there. He was standing just inside, nevertheless, when she entered, and his expression was a cross between vicious anger and bleary drunkenness. Tish's guard immediately went up. Larry seldom drank, and did not hold his liquor well when he did.

'Hello, Larry,' she said as calmly as she could manage. 'This is a surprise. I forgot you had a key. What are you doing here?'

'Just waiting to see how long you'd stay out there with old scar-face,' he replied. 'I need to talk to you.'

'Larry, I think I said everything I have to say to you this morning,' Tish replied. She casually removed her coat and hung it up, then opened a cupboard and poured some cat food into Rocky's bowl.

'Maybe you ought to listen to me for a while,' Larry said, 'especially after this!' His voice exploded in anger on the last word, and Tish looked to see him pounding on the page of the *Laketown Herald* where the item about her Thanksgiving visit to Nicholas was printed.

Tish eyed him warily from across the table. There was something frightening about seeing him this way, his usually neatly combed hair unkempt, his face flushed. 'I put that item there for a purpose,' she said. 'I knew people would spread the word and get it all wrong, so I simply confirmed their suspicions and took the bite away. They know now they have my permission to talk about me and Nicholas, which takes away a lot of the fun.'

Larry leaned on the table and glared at her. 'Are you crazy? Don't you know the kind of things they'll say about you for getting involved with him? What they'll say about me for having lost you to that miserable...'

'Larry!' Tish said warningly. 'That's enough!' She might have known it was his own bruised ego that was motivating him more than any concern about her!

'Oh, no,' Larry said, shaking his head. 'I want to know why you're doing this.' He began moving around the table towards Tish. 'I want to know what that man's got that I don't have, aside from his money, because I know you and it isn't the money you're after.'

'He's just ... different,' Tish said, sidling away, her heart beginning to pound in fear.

'Different? I'll say he's different,' Larry sneered. 'Tell me, what is it like to kiss that ugly so-and-so? Or does he do more than kiss you? Do you like to be overpowered and made love to? Is that it?'

'No!' Tish screamed at the same moment that Larry lunged for her. 'Let go of me!' she cried, trying to pull herself free but failing. Larry's grip was like iron, cruelly digging into her arm. 'You're wrong, Larry,' she said hoarsely, scarcely able to breathe in the face of Larry's wild stare. 'He doesn't do that. He wouldn't! Let go of me, right now. Please!'

Larry shook his head. 'No, Tish,' he said, his eyes glittering with something more like hatred than love. 'I'm going to kiss you now and I'm going to find out what it takes to turn you on. If it takes more than kissing, I'm going to find that out, too!'

'No!' Tish screamed again, pushing at him with all of her might and twisting from side to side. 'Let go of me. Go away! Go away! Go away! Help!'

Like an explosion, the door suddenly flew open with such force that the glass window shattered.

'Let go of her!' came the order that resounded like a clap of thunder.

Larry turned, startled. His hands fell immediately to his sides and his face turned ghostly pale.

'Nicholas!' Tish cried. 'Thank God!'

She watched, trembling but fascinated, as Nicholas advanced on Larry, his eyes so black with fury that for a moment she feared he might kill the smaller man. He reached out and took hold of Larry's throat just long enough to make Larry uncertain of his intentions, then slid his hand down to grasp Larry's collar instead.

'Don't-ever-come-near-Tish-again,' he said in deep, staccato tones. When Larry only stared at him, Nicholas picked him up with one hand and gave him a shake. 'Do you understand?' he roared. 'Because, if you do, so help me I'll do everything to you that I'm only thinking of doing right now!'

Larry nodded. His teeth were chattering with fear, but his eyes were narrow slits of hatred. Nicholas walked him towards the door, never releasing his grip. With his other hand he grabbed up Larry's coat from the chair where Larry had tossed it, shoved it into Larry's hands, then released him with a motion that propelled Larry through the door.

'Get out,' he said, giving the other man one last look of utter contempt.

Larry scurried down the steps. 'I'll get you for this,' he called back as distance gave him courage. 'Just you wait and see. I'll get you.'

Nicholas only snorted contemptuously. He closed the door, gave a perfunctory glance to the pile of glass, then quickly turned and gathered Tish into his arms.

'Are you all right, sweet love?' he asked softly. When she made no reply, only burrowed against him, sobbing, he answered himself. 'No, you're not,' he said. He picked her up and carried her into the living-room, turned on a lamp, then sat down with her in his arms. 'There, there, it's all right now,' he murmured, stroking her hair as if she were a child. 'No one's going to hurt you, not ever, as long as there's a breath in my body.'

Slowly the warmth of Nicholas's loving embrace crept into Tish's taut body. She began to relax and her sobs subsided.

'How did you ever know to come just when you did?' she asked, looking up at him through still tearful eyes.

'I used to be famous for being in the right place at the right time,' Nicholas replied with a smile. 'I guess I still have the knack. I felt something was wrong when you left, that you were still angry with me and we needed to talk it out. Your kiss didn't feel right, somehow. I knew I wouldn't be able to sleep, so I decided to come to you for a change. When I saw the other car in your driveway, I almost turned around and went home, but then I realised that someone had been here before you. That didn't seem right, so I decided to find out what was going on.'

'Thank God you did,' Tish said, shuddering. 'I had no idea that Larry would ever do such a thing. He was always so terribly proper and restrained. That was the reason my father liked him. Wait until he hears about what happened tonight!'

Nicholas grimaced. 'One of the things that was bothering me earlier was what your father will think of me as a son-in-law. When you mentioned that he owned the newspaper, I suddenly remembered that he's a retired colonel. He's apt to find my record somewhat wanting.'

'Oh, Nicholas,' Tish said with a tired sigh, 'I don't give a darn what he thinks.' She nestled her cheek against his neck and stroked his shoulder meditatively. 'He's not an easy man to please,' she said, 'but I think that once he gets to know you he'll be happy for us both. Hearing how you rescued me tonight isn't going to hurt any, either. Now that I'm able to think about it, it was really wonderful the way you came dashing to the rescue, like a knight of old. Too bad you couldn't have come riding in on Titan.' She sat up and smiled, expecting an answering sparkle in Nicholas's clear, blue eyes. Instead he made a wry grimace.

'Too bad no one else sees me as a hero,' he said.

'Oh, but there is someone else who does,' Tish said, deciding that this was the perfect time to tell her story about Charlie. When she had finished and asked if Nicholas knew anyone at all by that name, he shook his head.

'No,' he said. 'Not that I can remember. It doesn't change things, anyway, but it does help a little. At least I apparently did one thing right.'

Tish frowned thoughtfully. Was this the time to inject her doubts about Mike O'Hara's story? Well, why not? After seeing Nicholas in action tonight, she was more sure than ever that he was no coward.

'Nicholas,' she said, placing both hands on his shoulders and leaning towards him, 'I want to tell you something, and I want you to take it seriously. I don't believe Mike O'Hara's story. I don't know why he would lie to you, but I think he did. I felt it even before I got to know you, that night when he told everyone at the party. Hal never let him tell it before, you know, and he was furious when he did. Mavis says she doesn't think Hal believed it, either. And I think if we could ever find Charlie, he might have an entirely different story to tell.'

Nicholas shook his head. 'I appreciate the loyalty of friends,' he said, 'but Mike had all of the details down so well that I can't really doubt it, no matter how much I'd like to. As for finding Charlie...' He shrugged. 'I wouldn't know where to begin.'

'Well, I'm going to find him,' Tish said with sudden determination.

'Good luck,' Nicholas said with a sceptical lift of his brows. 'When you're through with that, I have a haystack that has a needle in it somewhere.' He smiled. 'Don't look so dejected. I believe you'll try. Maybe even succeed. But right now, how about us working on some easier problems while you finish unwinding from your scare? I don't want you thinking I have a heart of granite, you know.'

'I know you don't,' Tish said, snuggling close to him again. 'But about old Eben...' She told Nicholas what Stanley had told her, and he quickly promised to look into the matter and do everything he could for the man, including putting him on paid leave-of-absence, instead of firing him, so that he could be with his wife. 'I think your heart is a big, soft marshmallow,' Tish said, pleased at his response. 'Now, about my quitting the newspaper...'

They discussed the pros and cons of Tish's continuing at her work, finally agreeing that it would be best for her to begin training someone to take over the major part of the work, but that she could keep a hand in as long as she wanted to.

'Let's plan to be married on Valentine's Day,' Tish suggested, when that question arose. 'It sounds so romantic, and should give us enough time to get ready.'

'What about your father?' Nicholas reminded her.

'He'll be home for Christmas,' Tish said. 'We won't announce it formally until we've told him in person, but

I'm going to tell him right away so he can start adjusting to the idea.'

'No, Tish,' Nicholas said firmly. 'I want to ask him for your hand. It may sound old-fashioned, but I'd prefer it that way, and I think your father would too.'

Tish started to object, then looked into Nicholas's eyes and read the love and concern there.

'All right, my love,' she agreed. 'That does sound rather nice.' She yawned and looked at her watch. 'Good heavens, it's almost four o'clock.'

'You run along to bed,' Nicholas said. 'I'll patch up your door and then curl up on your sofa. I'm not leaving you alone here tonight.' He frowned. 'Of course, if someone sees my car out in front...'

'Don't worry about it,' Tish interrupted. 'The whole town probably thinks we're sleeping together already. May as well get in bed with me and make it true. I'm too tired to make love, anyway.'

Nicholas chuckled. 'So am I. Besides, I already decided to put that off until we're officially married. Let's do this whole thing right, even if no one else thinks we are.'

'You've decided?' Tish raised her eyebrows. 'Well, all right, Sir Lancelot, if you insist. But don't blame me if you don't get credit for your virtue.' She leaned forward and kissed Nicholas on the chin. 'Let's secede from the human race, just you and me. It gets so tiresome, worrying about who thinks what.'

'What do you think I was trying to do until you came along?' Nicholas asked with a wry little smile.

CHAPTER NINE

TISH felt as if she had only slept a few winks when the telephone beside her bed rang. Nicholas, sprawled beside her, groaned. Who on earth could it be? she wondered, trying to reach the phone without moving, and failing. Nicholas muttered a few words in his sleep.

'I'll get it in the kitchen,' Tish said, pushing herself from the bed. She swayed dizzily, then staggered into her kitchen, grabbed the telephone from its receiver, and sank into a chair. 'Hello?' she croaked hoarsely.

'Letitia,' came the roar of her father's voice, grating with displeasure, 'I want some answers from you!'

Oh, lord, Tish thought grimly. What now? She listened, appalled, as her father told her of receiving a telephone call in the night from Larry Johnson, in which all of the facts of the previous night's events were reversed, making him the hero. Not only that, but he had told her father of the newspaper item, saying it had made Tish the laughing-stock of Laketown. By the time he had finished, Tish was so angry that she was shaking.

'All right, now hear this!' she shouted, when her father had once again demanded an explanation. She went through all of the events that had happened between her and Larry over the past weeks, concluding with a vivid description of the previous night that left her father gasping in shock.

'The man's lost his mind!' he said, horrified. 'Stay away from him.'

'I'm trying to!' Tish snapped.

'Now, what is all this about you and Nicholas Morgan?' her father asked.

'I love him, that's what!' Tish shouted, banging the receiver down. She looked up to see Nicholas standing in the doorway, blinking sleepily.

'Your father?' he asked.

Tish nodded. 'You'll never guess what happened,' she said, then told him.

'Good lord,' he said, repeating her father's opinion that Larry had gone over the edge. 'I'm going to stick to you like glue until the man calms down.'

'I'll be all right at the newspaper office,' Tish said. She looked up at her large kitchen clock. 'I'd better get ready to go.' She started to stand, then sank back down, clutching her head. 'Oooh,' she moaned. 'My head hurts.'

Nicholas was at her side in an instant, laying his cool hand on Tish's forehead. 'You've got a fever,' he said immediately, lifting her chin and peering into her face. 'Open your mouth and stick out your tongue.'

'I'm all right,' Tish protested, but did as instructed.

'Red as a beet,' Nicholas said. 'Swallow. Does it hurt?'

'A little,' Tish lied, for it had been very painful.

'A little, my foot,' Nicholas scolded. 'Back to bed with you, my girl.'

'But I can't,' Tish wailed, feeling like crying. 'I'll be all right...' She tried to stand, but the world began to whirl around her and she clutched at the table for support. Nicholas picked her up bodily and carried her back to her bed.

'Go back to sleep, beautiful one,' he said, tucking the covers around her.

'But, the *Herald*...'

'I'll take care of everything,' Nicholas said. 'Believe it or not, I can even cope with that.' He picked up the telephone and dialled a number. 'Titus,' he said, 'leave those blasted gates open and come to Letitia's house. I have something far more precious for you to guard.' That done, he reached down and unplugged the bedside phone. 'Just to keep you honest,' he said, grinning down at Tish's disgruntled frown. He bent and kissed Tish on the forehead. 'Sleep,' he ordered in a soft but firm voice.

'All right,' Tish said faintly. Everything looked so fuzzy, anyway, that she could hardly keep her eyes open. And it was so wonderful to have someone say they could take care of everything. No one had said that to her in a very long time.

For the rest of that morning, Tish faded in and out of a deep sleep, rousing only enough to occasionally be aware that someone was in the room with her. She thought she saw Titus and Mavis and Nicholas, but could not be sure. Then, in early afternoon, she was roused more firmly. Nicholas was there with the local doctor, who never, as far as Tish knew, made house calls. Nicholas certainly could take care of things! The doctor poked and prodded and peered at her throat, then gave her a shot and ordered her to stay in bed until he told her otherwise.

'But...' Tish began, then looked over the doctor's shoulder at Nicholas, who had one eyebrow raised in warning. 'Yes, sir,' Tish replied weakly.

For the rest of the day she was dimly conscious of someone, usually Mavis, appearing with a glass of water and a bent straw, ordering her to drink and swallow a tablet. It was the next morning when she finally awoke, her throat still raw, but her head almost clear. She raised up on her elbows and looked around.

'Is anyone here?' she said faintly.

Nicholas appeared at the door immediately. 'I am,' he said. 'Are you feeling better?'

Tish nodded, staring at Nicholas. He was straightening his necktie, already dressed in a dark suit and white shirt. She had never seen him dressed that way before, and the effect was stunning. He looked so handsome that tears came to Tish's eyes.

'You look wonderful,' she said huskily. 'Where are you going?' She stared, entranced, as Nicholas came and sat on the edge of her bed.

'To meet your father at the airport in Rochester,' he replied, bending to give her a kiss. He sat back and smiled. 'I thought I should try to make a good impression.'

'My...my father?' Tish croaked.

'Your father,' Nicholas affirmed. 'He called yesterday afternoon. He's worried about Johnson, and wants to be here to protect you. I agreed that it was an excellent idea.'

'Oh.' Tish sank back against her pillows. 'Then you talked to him?' she asked.

'Some,' Nicholas replied. 'I gathered he wanted to interview me a bit. I told him I wanted to marry you. It seemed a good idea, under the circumstances.'

Tish swallowed painfully, wondering if the new ache in her stomach was from her virus or her father's impending visit. Her eyes searched Nicholas's face, wondering if he was as anxious about her father's queries as she was. He did not look at all disturbed.

'You don't look very worried about meeting my father,' Tish commented.

Nicholas shrugged. 'I'm a little anxious about it, but it doesn't bother me a lot. I'll do whatever has to be done to convince him I'm the man for you. I'm no...' he paused, then smiled crookedly. 'Coward,' he concluded.

'I know you're not,' Tish said, tears of happiness coming to her eyes. 'I've always known it.'

'I think you're more than a little prejudiced,' Nicholas said. He kissed Tish's cheek again. 'Get over that virus so I can kiss you the way I want to,' he murmured in her ear.

When Nicholas had gone, Tish lay very still, suffused in a warm glow that had nothing to do with her fever. It was a glow from knowing that Nicholas was beginning to believe in himself again. The glow faded. If only her father would give him a chance...

Mavis arrived and began plying Tish with juices and gelatines. 'Doctor's orders,' she said firmly, when Tish tried to plead that she was too nervous over her father's arrival to eat anything. 'Besides, you don't need to worry. That's quite a man you've got. He can get out the *Herald* as well as you can.' She handed Tish a copy of the previous day's paper.

'He certainly can,' Tish said after scanning the issue. 'I wonder where he learned that?'

'He and Hal used to edit the high school newspaper,' Mavis replied. 'He got Hal to help him yesterday, and Hal's working on it today. I'm almost glad you got sick so the two of them got together again. They were having a wonderful time.'

'I think it would have happened soon, anyway,' Tish said. Nicholas was ready to face the world again, scars and all.

She closed her eyes and tried to rest, but could only doze for a few moments at a time, every sound awakening her. At last she heard the outside door open, her father's voice greeting Titus, and then a single set of footsteps coming towards her room. She turned her head and smiled nervously as her father's square, militarily erect form appeared in her doorway.

'Hello, Dad,' she said. 'It's awfully good of you to come back just to protect me.'

Neil Holmsworth advanced to his daughter's bed, bent precisely, and kissed her on the forehead. He cleared his throat. 'I'm not just here to protect you,' he said. 'There seems to be a lot going on here that I didn't know about.'

Tish studied her father's face. He did not look especially upset, but with him it was hard to tell. He did not believe that military men should indulge in emotional displays.

'I guess you might say that,' Tish said noncommitally. 'Where's Nicholas?'

'He went to help Hal Greer with the *Herald*. I'm going over there myself in a few minutes. Putter around the old place a bit. Then, later this evening, I am going to Castlemont for some discussions with Mr...er—Nicholas.' He made a little harrumphing sound. 'Nicholas sent you his love and said to tell you he would see you tomorrow. He thought we might like some time alone to talk, and the rest of the time you should sleep.' Neil Holmsworth bent and peered at Tish. 'How are you feeling today? Has the doctor been here yet?'

'No, but I'm feeling much better,' Tish replied. 'Sit down.' She took a deep breath and crossed her fingers beneath the bedcovers. 'Tell me what you think of Nicholas.' She watched apprehensively as her father sat stiffly on a small straight chair.

'Interesting man,' Neil Holmsworth replied, giving Tish a brief glance. He pulled his pipe from his pocket, tamped it with his finger, and then lighted it. After a few puffs, he went on, 'I'm not ready to approve of your marrying him yet, though,' he said, peering thoughtfully through his cloud of smoke at Tish. 'Not that I think it will stop you if I don't. However, I do appreciate Mr. . . er—Nicholas's desire to have my approval. That is one of the main reasons I wish to talk to him this evening, in spite of his unfortunate career in the military.'

'He already told you about that?' Tish asked hoarsely. Good heavens! If that wasn't taking the bull by the horns!

'Yes. Yes, he did. Of course, Johnson made some allusions to his cowardice, but I discounted that after I talked to you. However, I have a great many questions now. A great many.'

Tish swallowed painfully. Poor Nicholas. She remembered only too well that, when her father asked questions, it was rather like being a dummy on a target range. He asked them rapid fire, staccato, and repeatedly, even if all you had done was pull up a flower seedling by mistake instead of a weed.

'Well, then,' Neil Holmsworth rose, perpetually at attention. 'I'm going to find something to eat in the kitchen and then go to the *Herald*. You get some sleep, young lady. You look dreadful.'

'Yes, sir,' Tish replied, smiling weakly. She submitted to another kiss on her forehead, then closed her eyes. Oh, how she wished that she might sleep for a hundred years and then wake up to find her prince bending over her, all of their problems solved!

By that evening, Tish was feeling enough better to eat some regular food. Her father took his dinner on a tray in her room, talking amiably about his work on the Indians of the South-west, but evading Tish's attempts to find out any details of what he wanted to question Nicholas about. He put her off by saying that it involved 'a lot of military jargon' that she would not understand.

'Be kind to Nicholas,' Tish pleaded when her father was ready to leave. He raised his eyebrows at her.

'I am interested in facts, Letitia,' he said. 'Facts are neither kind nor unkind.'

Tish sighed, knowing that it would be no use to press him further. When he had gone, she went into the living room where Titus was watching television, and curled up on the sofa beneath a warm blanket, too anxious to stay in the quiet of her room and read. The television programme could not hold her interest long, either.

'This is driving me crazy!' she finally exclaimed, sitting up and pushing her hair back from her forehead with a clammy hand. 'I can't just sit here and not know what's going on!'

'Now, Letitia, just be calm,' Titus said. 'You know the doctor said you should stay in bed for at least another day.'

'If I do, I'll be a basket case,' Tish replied. She got to her feet, suddenly determined to find out what was transpiring at Castlemont. She was not about to let her father destroy all of the progress that Nicholas had made, no matter how well intentioned he might be on behalf of his only daughter.

'Go and get the car warmed up, Titus,' she said. 'You're taking me to Castlemont.'

'Oh, no, Letitia...'

'Oh, yes! I'll put on my warmest clothes. I'll be all right, really I will. And if you won't do it, I'll drive myself,' she warned, seeing that Titus was about to protest further.

Grumbling about her stubbornness, Titus got to his feet, and Tish quickly went to her room and got into warm, woolly clothing, followed by her heavy parka, boots, and furry mittens.

'I'm ready,' she told Titus, who was hovering by the door, looking extremely uncomfortable. 'Don't worry, Titus,' she told him, 'they won't blame you. They both know me.'

Both Nicholas and her father proved her statement shortly thereafter, when Winchell had reluctantly ushered her into the library at Castlemont, where a fire was blazing in the fireplace, sending flashes of light reflecting from the myriad colours of the books and the deeply glowing old woods. Tish could see her father pacing back and forth, head down, puffing on his pipe, as if he were lord of the castle, while Nicholas sat in a chair beyond him. It looked, Tish thought, far too cosy a room for a bitter discussion of Nicholas's cowardice. She advanced into the room.

'Hello, Father,' she said.

'Letitia! What are you doing here?' Her father stopped pacing and fixed Tish with a look that would have made her cringe in her younger days. Now she simply raised her chin and looked straight back at him, beginning to remove her outer clothing.

'I've come to find out what's going on,' she replied. 'And don't tell me to leave, because I won't.'

Neil Holmsworth glared at his daughter, then turned to Nicholas. 'Can you do anything with her?' he asked.

Tish nearly burst out laughing at the suppressed laughter she saw in Nicholas's eyes. His lips were twitching, but he managed a sober, 'Not a thing, sir. She's a very determined woman.'

'Very well,' the colonel said, as if he still had control
of the situation. He pointed to a chair by the hearth.
'Sit down there, Letitia, where you'll be warm. And be
quiet.'

'Yes, sir,' Tish said, blowing a kiss to Nicholas behind
her father's back. She sat down, watching curiously, as
her father began to pace back and forth again, puffing
harder than ever on his pipe. Nicholas was sitting on the
edge of a large, red leather chair, leaning forward and
watching her father attentively. His expression was intense, as if he were trying to see into the older man's
mind.

'Let's go through that bit one more time,' her father
said, apparently picking up where they had been interrupted. 'The story is that the point man...' He looked
over at Nicholas.

'Went fifty yards due south and met no resistance,'
Nicholas finished quickly. 'I then ordered Kevin O'Hara
and his buddy, Frank Baum, to circle to his right...'

For a long time, Tish listened and watched intently.
Her father would nod, then ask for a repetition of some
precise fact. She could not imagine what he could be
getting from the story, for much of it made no sense to
her, just as he had warned. Finally her father stopped
pacing, knocked the ashes from his pipe into a large
ashtray, and shook his head. Her heart sank. He could
find nothing wrong with the story. Then, to her
amazement, she was proved wrong.

'It's too pat,' her father said, looking over at Nicholas.
'Entirely too much detail. Even a very experienced
combat soldier, when he gets in a situation like that,
can't know everything that's going on within fifty yards
or more. In fact, he's lucky if he knows where he is
himself.' He shook his head again. 'No, Nicholas, my

boy, I don't believe it. Either Mike O'Hara embroidered tremendously on some basic facts, or else the whole thing is a fabrication.'

Nicholas stared down at the intricate pattern of the oriental rug on the floor in front of him. 'I guess I'll never know which it is, will I?' he said in a low voice.

'Maybe you will if we can find Charlie,' Tish put in.

Neil Holmsworth turned and frowned at her. 'Charlie? Charlie who?'

Tish related once again her story of the man who had called Nicholas Morgan the bravest man he ever knew.

'Hmm,' her father said when she had finished, at last sitting down. 'Must have been someone who came up that day on some special detail. Mike O'Hara should know who he was.'

'Mavis thought of that, too,' Tish said, 'but I'd hate to approach him on it. If he has some reason for lying, and thought we were going to find out the truth, he might track down Charlie and pay him not to tell what he knows. With the money Mike has now, he could pay a lot, and Charlie didn't look very prosperous.'

'I could easily double anything that Mike could come up with,' Nicholas said. He grinned when Tish looked at him, startled.

'Yes, I suppose you could,' she said. 'I never thought of that.'

The colonel shook his head. 'Let's not get into bribery,' he said. 'It could get ugly. I still have some contacts in the military. I'll see what I can find out.' He frowned at his daughter. 'I'd better take you home. You should be there in bed right now.'

Tish sighed and bit her lip. Her father had been quite kind to Nicholas, but nothing was resolved. 'I know,' she said, 'but . . . but Dad, what if we can't find Charlie? What about Nicholas and me?'

'Nicholas and you?' Her father looked as if he did not understand the question. 'Why, get married, of course. The sooner, the better. Wild horses couldn't stop you, so why should I try?'

At that, Tish let out a whoop that nearly destroyed her still raspy throat. She ran to her father and gave him a hug, then flung herself into Nicholas's arms, as he stood to shake her father's hand. She could feel his heart pounding, hear the catch in his voice as he said, 'Thank you, sir. I'll try to be worthy of your trust.'

'I'm sure you will be,' Neil Holmsworth replied, his usually crisp voice suspiciously husky.

As she and her father drove home together, Tish felt warm and happy, but still uncertain about one thing. Did her father believe that Nicholas could have done what Mike O'Hara accused him of doing? Facts. There were still not enough facts. But did her father have an opinion, an intuition? If he did, she was afraid he would be reluctant to tell her, lest he later be proven wrong. Admitting to error was not his strong suit. Still, maybe if she sneaked up on the topic, she might get some inkling. She laid her hand on her father's arm.

'You've made Nicholas and me very happy tonight, Dad,' she said. 'Thank you.'

'I'd be a fool to fight you,' he replied drily. Then he added, surprisingly, 'I like Nicholas. I'm inclined to believe that O'Hara made up his story.'

'Inclined to believe?' Tish chided him gently. 'What about the facts?'

Neil Holmsworth actually chuckled. 'I know one fact. Mike O'Hara's father used to cheat at poker.'

CHAPTER TEN

IT WAS heartwarming to Tish to see the way Nicholas's old friends welcomed him back into their midst. News of their engagement spread like wildfire, and even the townspeople smiled and nodded to them, their smiles no longer knowing and hateful but open and friendly. It was, she thought, as if they had only been waiting for Nicholas to smile back, as if once he did his scars disappeared for them, too, in the beautiful warmth of his blue eyes. She knew, too, that no small part of his acceptance was due to the fact that 'The Colonel' had welcomed him as a prospective son-in-law. 'The Colonel' knew about military things, and, if he thought Nicholas was all right, those other stories must be wrong.

Nicholas presented Tish with a stunning ring, a heart-shaped ruby surrounded by diamonds.

'For your warm, wonderful, indomitable heart,' he told her when he slipped it on to her finger. 'Without you, I'd still be the loneliest man in the world.' He kissed her tenderly, while she sobbed uncontrollably in his arms. 'Don't cry, love,' he whispered into her ear, 'or you'll make me cry, too.'

'Then d-don't make me so happy,' she replied. 'I love you so much, I think I'm going to explode.'

As the Christmas season approached, there were parties every weekend and, in between, Tish and Nicholas spent long, wonderful evenings together. The first snow melted, to be replaced by a softer, gentler snow that brought out all of the children's sleds to sail down the hills of Laketown. Tish and Nicholas went sledding, too, with Hal and Mavis and other old friends, acting like children again. One sunny Saturday, Nicholas drove a sleigh into town, pulled by a pair of mighty Clydesdales he had bought on a whim. He and Tish drove all around Laketown. Then, seeing the envious eyes of the children they passed, Nicholas stopped and gave rides to them for over an hour. Two little boys stood watching him help a little girl down from the sleigh after her ride. They were talking to each other in low voices, and then looking at Nicholas. Finally the smaller of the two came up to him.

'Hey, mister,' he said, pointing at Nicholas's face. 'How did you get those scars?'

Tish held her breath, but Nicholas only grinned at them.

'The doctors told me a grenade went off in my face,' he answered. 'I don't remember it, though.'

'Wow!' said the boy, impressed. 'You must be awful brave.'

Nicholas shook his head. 'No,' he replied. 'Just lucky to be here.'

Tish relaxed again. She knew there would be incidents like that, as long as Nicholas had his scars. Only she knew that he would keep them unless, or until, he learned definitely that he had not caused the death of his men. Her father had made a trip to Washington in search of any records that might provide the identity of the man named Charlie, but had come home frustrated and empty-handed.

'Blasted computers have the records of the battalion the man should have been in all fouled up. They said it could take months to straighten them out,' he complained. 'Things were better before they got those damned machines.'

Even though everyone in town already knew of the engagement, the Greer family insisted on giving Tish and Nicholas a special party to mark the event. They were ecstatic when Nicholas suggested they combine it with a New Year's Eve celebration and hold the party at Castlemont.

'That's only a month and a half before the wedding,' Tish pointed out. 'Do you think your staff can cope with two big bashes so close together? Some of them are getting along in years.'

'Just think how long they've had to rest since the last one,' Nicholas replied. 'But you're right, we are going to have to hire some younger blood. Especially when the children come along.'

'Oh? Do you think our children are going to be that wild?' she teased.

'With you for a mother, what else could they be?' he teased back.

Christmas came and went, the happiest Tish could remember since her mother had died. Nicholas proclaimed it the happiest he could ever remember. He had reluctantly forgone any elaborate Christmas decorations at Castlemont, since Mavis and her mother had already begun making preparations for the New Year's Eve party. It was to be the most lavish affair that Laketown had seen in many a year, with dancing in the grand salon and enough refreshments in the banquet hall to feed the entire town, if they chose to come. And they were all invited.

'I'm not sure about this,' Tish said, when she saw the notice that Nicholas wanted printed in the *Herald*. 'I mean, I think it's a grand gesture, but where will everyone park? And what if...what if Larry Johnson comes?'

'There's plenty of room to park,' Nicholas replied calmly, 'and I doubt if Johnson will show up. I've only seen him a couple of times since that night, and each time he turned around and walked the other way.'

'All right, you're the boss,' Tish said. 'Don't blame me if all your shrubs get trampled.' She leaned over and kissed Nicholas on the neck. 'But I'd rather be alone with you.'

'And I with you, lovely lady,' Nicholas replied, 'but, hey, I don't plan to get engaged ever again.'

Tish smiled, her heart melting at the adoration she saw in Nicholas's eyes. She couldn't fault him for wanting to have parties and celebrate now. It had been a long time for him, too. Far too long.

December the thirty-first in Laketown dawned cloudy and cold, a light snow falling, but by afternoon the skies had cleared, leaving a coating of white perfection on the old snow and a stillness in the air that seemed as if the whole town were waiting, breathless, for the party. Tish had an elegant dress of green silk that matched her eyes. She thought for a time of wearing her ridiculous green wig when she first arrived at the party, to remind Nicholas of the night they had met, but decided against it when her father declared it the most awful-looking thing he had ever seen.

Promptly at eight o'clock, Tish and her father, resplendent in his dress uniform, arrived at Castlemont. Nicholas greeted them at the door, so tall and handsome and elegant that Tish could only stare at him, unable to believe that he was truly her husband-to-be. He and her father exchanged a smart salute, a gesture that touched

Tish's heart. She could see that a warm affection was growing between her two favourite men.

'You,' she told Nicholas when she took his arm, 'are going to have trouble fighting off the women tonight. They will all be vying for a chance to dance with you, before I take you out of circulation permanently.'

Nicholas shook his head. 'My love, I already am,' he said, gallantly kissing her hand and then pulling her into his arms for a kiss that left her giddy.

Soon other guests began to arrive, at first in a trickle, then in an avalanche. By ten minutes before midnight, when Tish and Nicholas mounted the orchestra dais to formally announce their engagement, the hall was crowded. When Nicholas said that Letitia Prudence Holmsworth had agreed to make him the happiest man on earth, there was thunderous applause. Then, while the orchestra played Auld Lang Syne, everyone watched a special clock on the wall as the seconds ticked down to the New Year, greeting its arrival with blasts from the toy horns and noisemakers with which they had been provided.

The party went on for another hour, and then the guests began to leave. Tish and Nicholas were standing on the steps, saying goodbye to Mayor Braman of Laketown and his wife, when suddenly there came a sound like rolling thunder.

'What's that?' Tish said, turning to look up at Nicholas.

Before he could answer, there was an explosion of such force that the steps beneath them shook. Mrs Braman screamed, but Tish could make no sound. She was looking where Nicholas was looking, at the sky behind the house, where a red glow was lighting the sky. The stables were on fire.

'Call the fire department,' Nicholas said, before bolting in the direction of the stables at a run.

Tish ran back inside, discovering quickly that the fire department had already been notified. She tore off her dainty sandals and grabbed the first coat and pair of boots that she could find, then ran back outside. Men were already running up and down the drive, calling out, 'Keep the drive clear! Keep the drive clear for the fire engines!' She lifted her long skirt and ran towards the back of the house.

What she saw when she rounded the corner made her heart almost stop. Flames were shooting from the roof of the building, smoke billowing from every side. There were screams from the frightened horses and shouts from the men, whose shadowy forms she could see struggling in and out of the flames. As she drew near she could see Nicholas emerging from the building, Lady Whirlwind in tow. He handed the horse's bridle to Stanley, then disappeared once again into the cauldron.

'Oh, Nicholas!' Tish cried, standing still a short distance from the stables, her hands clenched at her sides and tears streaming down her face. 'No, Nicholas, no!' Surely no one could go into that inferno and survive? Oh, why didn't the fire engines get here? Other men came out, swatting at their burning clothing and shaking their heads. Finally Nicholas appeared, a towel over his head, leading another favourite mare. Again he handed it to the groom, who led it away. 'Nicholas, no!' Tish screamed, seeing that he was heading for the stable door again. He did not hear her, but plunged back into the fiery interior. Tish screamed his name again, and started to run towards him, but a hand caught her arm. It was her father.

'You can't help him, Tish,' he said. 'Just try to stay calm and pray.'

Just then the fire engines finally arrived, and Tish watched her father hurry to them and point towards the stable. Moments later, a man dressed in protective clothing and a mask rushed in where Nicholas had disappeared. Tish stood perfectly still, waiting, feeling as if an unreal silence had settled over only her. As far as she could tell, her heart had stopped beating and she was not breathing. It seemed like an eternity was passing. A beam collapsed, hissing, in the streams of water now playing on the fire. Then, struggling beneath the weight, the fireman emerged with Nicholas's body across his shoulders. He staggered forwards and laid the motionless form on a waiting stretcher.

'Nicholas!' Tish screamed once more, and then the world went black.

When Tish regained consciousness she was lying in a hospital bed, strapped down, a tube dripping fluids into her arm. She opened her eyes slowly, afraid the terrible visions that never seemed to stop would still be there. Instead, she saw only the gentle face of her father. He smiled.

'Welcome back,' he said.

Tish lifted her head and looked down at her body. 'Why am I strapped down like this?' she asked. 'Why am I here?'

'You were screaming and thrashing about,' her father replied, 'and you've been in deep shock. But I'll be able to take you home in a day or two.'

'Oh.' Tish laid her head back. In her mind's eye she could still see Nicholas's body being placed on the stretcher as clearly as if it were etched there. Tears ran from her eyes and she looked at her father, pleading silently. He understood, and reached out and took her hand in his.

'Nicholas is in the burns unit,' he said, 'getting the finest care possible. There is no definite answer yet, but with every minute that passes, his chances improve. I've been calling every half-hour to check on him.'

'How long has it been?' Tish whispered. It seemed it could have been only minutes, or as long as a year.

'Thirty-seven hours,' her father replied.

'I see,' Tish said, slowly absorbing the fact that Nicholas was not dead, but was in mortal danger still, and that while she had been lying here, helpless, he was fighting for his life without her. She felt a surge of determination flood through her weakened body. 'I've got to go to him, Dad,' she said. 'I can't stay here.'

Neil Holmsworth shook his head firmly. 'You must stay until the doctors say you're well enough to leave. What you've been through is very serious in itself.'

Tish read the determination on his face, and set her own mouth in a grim line. 'All right,' she said. 'What do I have to do to get better in record time?'

'Just keep that attitude, young lady,' said the doctor, coming into the room, 'and we'll have you on your feet in no time.' He removed Tish's constraints, checked her over thoroughly, and then left again, promising to get her moving as quickly as possible.

Tish looked back at her father and sighed. 'I wasn't much help, was I? Standing there, screaming and crying, when I could have tried to stop Nicholas.'

'I doubt you could have,' her father replied. 'Those horses meant the world to him.'

'Are they... all gone? I thought I saw Nicholas bring two out.'

'He did. And someone else brought another. Three mares were saved.'

Tish felt her tears begin again. Nicholas's beloved Titan, then, was gone. 'The fire...do they know how it started?' she asked.

Her father's face became grim. 'A propane leak in one of the heaters. They're not sure yet how it happened. It was probably a malfunctioning valve, or it could have been deliberate.' At Tish's horrified look, he shook his head. 'I thought immediately of Johnson's threat, too, so I called Hal and asked him to check into the man's whereabouts. I didn't want to make any false accusations.'

'And?' Tish prompted.

'Larry's been at his father's side in the coronary care unit here for several days. He's been enquiring about you and Nicholas regularly since he heard about the fire.'

Tish felt a great wave of relief. 'Poor Larry,' she sobbed. 'I guess I shouldn't have immediately suspected him. He's not that bad a person.'

'I don't think it was unreasonable of you,' her father replied. 'Jealousy can be a terrible thing. It has started wars and destroyed whole nations. Now, stop that crying, Letitia. It will only delay your recovery.'

Tish gulped and stopped. 'Yes, sir!' she said.

In only twenty-four hours, Tish was as near to Nicholas's side as she could get, outside the glass wall which enclosed his special room.

Nicholas lay silent and still, in a sterile environment to protect him from infection, so many tubes and monitors attached to him that Tish could scarcely see his face. It was with relief that she saw that his face had not been badly burned. She loved his dear face, and the scars that, for her, marked him as a very special man.

She did not care if he never had them changed. She counted the passing hours, watching the faces of the doctors and nurses as they came and went for some clue, afraid to ask very often lest they tell her something she did not want to hear. When seventy-two hours had passed, a young doctor suddenly tapped Tish on the shoulder.

'He'll make it,' he said simply, when Tish turned around.

'Thank you,' she said, blinking back her tears. She had sworn that if Nicholas were permitted to live she would never scream or cry again. It was so foolish, so useless, and in spite of what her father said she would always think that she might have been some help to Nicholas that night if she hadn't been in such a panic. That night she finally let her father take her home.

A week went by, then another week. From her vantage point, Tish could see that Nicholas was awake now, but she was not allowed to go into his room. For some time she took it as a rule, but finally she asked his nurse, 'Why? Why can't I go in?'

'Mr Morgan does not want to see anyone,' the nurse replied.

'Not ... anyone?' Tish repeated.

The nurse shook her head.

'But ... but we're engaged to be married!' Tish cried.

The nurse pursed her mouth in an unhappy line. 'He said no one,' she said. 'No one at all.'

Tish grasped at the nurse's arms. 'He can't mean me,' she said, 'He can't. Please, please let me go in. Please let me talk to him.'

The nurse looked at Tish's tired, drawn face. She had seen the poor woman waiting there, day after day. 'All right,' she said with a sigh, 'but only for a few minutes.'

Trembling, her heart pounding, Tish pushed open the door and tiptoed to stand next to Nicholas's bed. His eyes were open, but he was staring straight ahead, looking at nothing.

'Nicholas?' Tish said tentatively. 'It's Tish.'

'I know you're there,' he replied. 'I thought I told them to keep you out.'

'But...why?' she asked, scarcely able to make a sound over the terrible constriction that had grasped at her throat.

'It's over,' he replied. 'The illusion.'

'Illusion?' Tish repeated. 'I don't understand.'

'Yes, you do,' Nicholas said. 'It was all an illusion. The illusion that I could have a happy life, like any ordinary man. It isn't meant to be, Tish. Go away. Leave me alone.'

'Oh, Nicholas, you're wrong!' Tish cried. 'The good things are just beginning!'

Nicholas moved his head slightly from side to side. 'No. They're all dead. All of the horses but three, all of the men but one. Go away, Tish. Find another man.'

Tish stood very still, fighting for control, her teeth clenched to prevent herself from either screaming or crying once more. Nicholas was right, she did understand. He had decided that the fire at the stables was an omen, an omen to tell him that Mike O'Hara had, after all, been right. An omen that told him that he was not entitled to happiness. Never mind that it now destroyed Tish Holmsworth's happiness in the process. Nicholas Morgan was going to retreat from the world once again. Or...he thought he was. Anger began to fuel Tish's tired body and drain away her urge to cry. She moved closer to Nicholas's bed, leaning over him and finally engaging his cold, hollow eyes with her own.

'I understand all right, Nicholas,' she snapped, 'but you won't get away with it. I wouldn't let you before, and I certainly won't this time. As far as I'm concerned, we are still engaged to be married. I don't want any other man, and I hadn't better hear of you getting near any other woman!'

Nicholas gave a short, harsh laugh. 'That's not likely. Get out, Tish.'

Tish glared at him, her fists clenched in frustration. 'All right, you stubborn idiot. But I'll be back. You can bet your life on that.' She whirled and strode angrily from the room. She would be back. As soon as she had found Charlie.

CHAPTER ELEVEN

'I DON'T know, Letitia,' her father said, his forehead wrinkled with a concerned frown. Tish had burst into the *Herald* office and announced Nicholas's new withdrawal from the world and her renewed determination to find the man named Charlie. 'You may have to face the fact that this latest blow is more than even Nicholas can endure. He's a very sensitive man.'

'Yes,' Tish replied, 'but he's also strong and tough and brave. Besides, I'll go crazy if I don't do something. I can't just sit on my hands and wait to see if he'll change his mind. And if I can find Charlie...no, not if, *when* I find Charlie, it will change everything, for ever, I know it will. I'll find him if I have to track down every Charlie in the United States and ask him if he knew Nicholas Morgan.'

Neil Holmsworth looked at his daughter's determined face. 'All right,' he said. 'Let's get started. I'll tackle military records again.'

'I'll do the veterans' organisations,' Hal Greer volunteered. 'State by state.'

'I can do half of those,' Jeff said. 'My dad's a legionnaire. He knows a lot of people.'

'Maybe we should check the veterans' hospitals,' Peggy Willson suggested. 'You said the man walked with a cane.'

'Good idea, Peggy,' Tish said. 'I hope you all can keep the paper running without me a little longer. I'm going to Chicago and see what I can find out. Maybe the man was registered at the same hotel as I was. Just because I never saw him again, it doesn't mean he wasn't. It's a big place.'

The next morning, Tish was in Chicago, pleading with the hotel manager to let her see their registration list for the day she saw the man named Charlie. She had to pour out her entire story before he finally relented, still muttering that it was entirely irregular for him to do so. Together, they went through the list, finding only two likely candidates, one man who had signed the register with the first initial 'C', and another with Charles. The manager insisted on listening while Tish placed calls to the men to be sure she wasn't going to harass them. In only fifteen minutes, she knew that neither was the man she sought. Fighting back useless tears, she looked at the manager.

'Were there any other organisations meeting here then?' she asked. 'He could have been just meeting some people here. He could live in Chicago somewhere.'

'I was going to suggest that,' the manager said, suddenly more sympathetic. 'Let's see. We had the Friends of Lake Trout, Local Number 506 of the Plumber's Union, the Midwestern Art Teachers...' He went on to list several more groups, jotting down the names and telephone numbers of the officers who had made the reservations. 'Good luck to you, young lady,' he said, handing the list to Tish. 'My heart goes out to you and your fiancé. It really does.'

'Thank you,' Tish said, sniffling, but still not crying. 'I'll go to my room and check out the ones that are local groups.'

For the rest of that day she made telephone calls, took taxis to places where she could pick up membership lists, then made more calls. Nowhere did she find the right man named Charlie. The next day she went home, only a few groups left to contact.

She found her father almost frothing at the mouth in frustration.

'I finally got the name of Nicholas's commanding officer,' he said, 'only to find out that he is still missing, the company records were lost, and, as far as I can find out, no one ever questioned Mike O'Hara.' He pounded the desk with his fist. 'That is a hell of a way to run an army!'

'Keep calm, Dad,' Tish said. 'Maybe Charlie will turn out to be one of the Midwestern Art Teachers.'

But he was not. It took several weeks to get their list, and several days to check out the possibilities on it. None was the right man. In the meantime, other lists were coming in, and the colonel had a second telephone installed in the *Herald* office so that the always busy phone would not prevent the local people from reaching their newspaper.

On many days, after calling number after number, Tish felt like crying until no more tears would come, but she did not give in. Nothing, she swore, would keep her from finding her man, not if it took her a year, two years, or the rest of her life. In late February she found out from Titus that Nicholas had returned to Castlemont, still pale and weak, but able to get around.

'How...how does he seem, Titus?' Tish asked.

Titus shook his head. 'Very low, Letitia, very low. If it weren't for Lady Whirlwind's expecting Titan's foal in the spring...' Tears came to the old man's eyes. 'The man's a stubborn fool, Letitia, a stubborn fool.'

It almost made Tish ill to think of Nicholas, alone in that huge mansion, needing her but unwilling to give in. Several times she thought of going to him, but stopped

herself, even though Titus told her he would never keep
her out, in spite of Nicholas's orders.

'Is there any message I could give him from you?'
Titus asked one day. 'I don't think he'd fire me for doing
that.'

'Tell him to keep his eyes open at all times,' Tish
suggested. 'One of these days he's going to see me
coming, and when I do, I'm not leaving again. And...tell
him that I love him and I'm still planning to marry him.'

Still, as February gave way to March, she began to
have her doubts. She was so tired of calling men named
Charles, only to find out they had never known Nicholas.
Perhaps, she thought grimly, that wasn't even the man's
real name. Maybe it was his middle name, not his first.
Maybe his friend called everyone 'Charlie'.

'I think you'd better give yourself a rest,' her father
said. 'You're getting too thin, too tired-looking. You
won't be able to keep this up indefinitely.'

'Oh, yes, I will,' Tish replied defiantly.

She had just that morning seen the first robin of spring
in the park when Peggy Willson came wheeling up the
ramp that Jeff had built so that she could get into the
Herald office and work as an assistant, too.

'Look at this, Tish,' Peggy said, pulling a Washington
D.C. newspaper from her book bag. 'My dad subscribes
to this paper, and there's a picture in here today that
looks like the man you described. Of course, it probably
isn't, but...' She handed the paper to Tish.

Tish took one look at the picture and burst into for-
bidden tears. 'It's him!' she cried. 'That's Charlie!'

The picture was of a bearded veteran, standing before
the Vietnam memorial, tears running down his cheeks
as he searched through the list of names inscribed on
the black stone. Underneath the picture the heading said

simply, 'A Michigan veteran searches for the name of a fallen comrade.' But best of all, Tish saw immediately, was that the name of the photographer was in the corner below the picture.

'If I can track down that photographer, he may have the man's name,' she said excitedly. 'Otherwise, we've at least got it narrowed down to Michigan. Let's hope that photographer hasn't decided to go off to Afghanistan or some other remote place!'

In minutes she had reached the city desk of the newspaper, and moments later was talking to the young photographer who had taken the picture.

'Do you know the man's name?' she asked. 'Please, it's terribly, terribly important that I find him.'

'Just a minute,' he replied. 'I think I've got it.'

'He thinks he's got it,' Tish said to the crowd who had gathered around her, all motion suspended. 'Yes. Yes, I've got it. Thank you. You've just saved my life.' She smiled at her father and her friends. 'The man's name is Charles Clinton. He's from Ann Arbor, Michigan. And right now I am going to call him. Unless, of course, he has an unlisted telephone.' She held up crossed fingers and called the information operator for Ann Arbor. 'The number for Charles Clinton, please,' she said. In seconds, a computer voice was telling her the number. In only a few more seconds, she had dialled it, her heart pounding so that her hand shook. A woman's voice answered.

'May I speak to Charles Clinton, please?' Tish said.

'May I tell him who is calling?' the woman replied.

'Tell him,' Tish said, 'that it is Letitia Holmsworth of the *Laketown Herald*, New York. I want to talk to him about Nicholas Morgan.'

The next voice that Tish heard was almost familiar, she had imagined hearing it so many times.

'Yes, Miss Holmsworth,' Charles Clinton said. 'I've thought of you often. Did you know Nicholas Morgan?'

'I do know Nicholas Morgan,' Tish replied. 'He wasn't killed, Mr Clinton. Just badly injured. Look, there's a very complicated story that I must tell you, and I can't do it over the telephone. Could I possibly come and see you? It's very, very important to me. And to Nicholas.'

'Why, yes. Certainly. When would you want to come?' Charles Clinton asked.

'Just as soon as I can get a flight,' Tish replied. 'I'll get a reservation and then call you back.' In only a few more minutes she was able to inform Charles Clinton that she would be at his home later that evening.

'Are you sure you'll be all right?' Neil Holmsworth asked anxiously, looking at his daughter's thin, pale face. She had said almost nothing since they had reached the airport, her expression so carefully blank that it seemed she was not there at all.

She looked at him and smiled briefly. 'I hope so,' she said softly. 'I'll know very soon, won't I?'

The Clintons' home was much more prosperous-looking than Tish had expected. A modern design in redwood and glass, it overlooked a pretty, woodsy glen. A friendly teenager ushered Tish into the spacious living-room and then went to find his parents. The Clintons came into the room together and welcomed Tish warmly. Laura Clinton was a strikingly pretty, dark-haired woman. Charles was the same slightly rumpled-looking man Tish had remembered. While they chatted for a few minutes, getting acquainted, Tish learned that Laura Clinton was an artist and Charles Clinton a professor of neuro-science at the university.

'We were in Chicago for an exhibition of Laura's paintings, and staying with friends,' Charles explained, when Tish told him of her futile search at the hotel. 'We had only stopped by there for dinner.' He smiled encouragingly at Tish. 'You said you had a very complicated, very important story to tell. Why don't you begin?'

'I scarcely know where to begin,' she replied, clutching her hands together nervously, 'but I guess the best place is the beginning.' She closed her eyes for a moment, her heart pounding. Dear lord, she thought, don't let me fall apart now. She took a deep breath. 'I hadn't seen Nicholas Morgan in many years. No one in Laketown had. Since the war. He stayed away from people. A recluse. Everyone thought it was because of his terrible scars. I was very surprised when you told me of his heroism. No one had ever mentioned it. Laketown is a small town, you see, and everyone gossips. Then one night I saw him. Mike O'Hara...' Tish paused, startled by the grim look that suddenly came over the face of Charles Clinton.

'Go on,' he said. 'What about O'Hara?'

'He had come to give a concert at Lakefront Park. I saw Nicholas there. I tried to talk to him. I knew he and Mike had been friends. All he said was that he didn't want me to mention he'd been there in the newspaper. Then he went away. Later, there was a party. Mike was there. Someone mentioned seeing Nicholas. Mike got very upset, very angry. He swore and called Nicholas names and said that he was a terrible coward. That he was responsible for Kevin O'Hara's being killed. He said he'd taken his platoon in the wrong direction...'

'That's patently ridiculous!' Charles Clinton inter-rupted vehemently. 'He couldn't have. He was al-ready...well, I thought he was dead. Surely, Nicholas has told someone what happened...' He stopped. Across the space of a coffee-table, seated in a comfortable chair, Tish Holmsworth had doubled forward, sobbing un-controllably, tears relieving months of tension streaming down her face.

'Oh, God,' she sobbed, 'I love him so. I knew he couldn't be a coward. I knew it all the time.'

Laura Clinton was immediately on her knees beside Tish, comforting her. 'It's all right, dear, go ahead and cry. We'll wait,' she said, patting Tish's hands, and then holding them in hers. 'Charlie,' she said over her shoulder, 'bring some tissues, will you? I have a feeling we're all going to need them.'

Slowly Tish regained control of herself. With encour-agement and many questions from the Clintons, she told her entire story.

'Could you tell me what really did happen?' she fi-nally asked Charlie Clinton.

'It's not a pretty story,' he replied. 'It actually begins a couple of days before the battle, when Nicholas and I were wounded. Mike O'Hara had disappeared, ap-parently gone AWOL. I was sent up to replace him. We held our position for about thirty-six hours, waiting for orders to move forward. Then, on the second morning, just as we were going to move out, O'Hara showed up. He was acting crazy. I didn't pay much attention. There was too much going on. Then, suddenly, someone yelled, "Look out!" There was a live grenade on the ground right between Lieutenant Morgan and me. Before I could move, Nicholas flung himself across that space and knocked me flat just as the grenade went off. It seemed to me afterwards that it all happened at exactly the same moment...the shout, the grenade going off, Nicholas landing on top of me. I was knocked unconscious and my leg was almost blown off. I thought he was dead. I kept fading in and out until the medics arrived, but he didn't move a muscle. He was so heavy, I couldn't get out from under him. When the medics did get there and picked him up, I heard one of them say, "I think this one's gone." I've assumed all this time that he was. Even when I couldn't find his name on the memorial, I did. I was going to write and ask someone why, but...you know how such things go.'

Tish had listened, spellbound, to Charlie's account, but a terrible chill went through her at what it seemed to imply.

'Are you saying,' she asked, 'that it was Mike O'Hara who threw that grenade between you and Nicholas?'

Charlie nodded, his face grim. 'Yes. And, I'm afraid, I left the ugliest detail out of my story.'

'What's that?' Tish whispered, almost afraid to find out.

'After the smoke and dust had cleared, O'Hara leaned over Morgan and me with the most evil look I've ever seen on a man. He said, "I guess it won't help you to be rich and handsome where you're going now, will it?" If I could have moved...'

Tears filled Tish's eyes again. 'And Nicholas thought Mike was his friend. But that certainly explains why Mike invented that story when he found out Nicholas was still alive.'

'I'm afraid it does,' Charlie agreed. He stood up. 'Well, shall we go?'

'Go?' Tish said hoarsely.

Charlie grinned. 'I think it's time Nicholas found out the truth, don't you? I fly my own plane now, so we can leave as soon as I call my research assistant to make some arrangements and file a flight plan.'

'But, Charlie,' Laura Clinton said gently, 'it's late. Tish is so tired. Why don't you wait until morning?'

'I won't be able to sleep, and I doubt Tish will, either.' He looked questioningly at Tish, who shook her head.

'Not a wink,' she replied.

'Good. Oh, one other thing, Tish. I'm something of an expert on memory. I work mostly with rats, but I know about humans, too. I don't think Nicholas's memory is absent, I think it's probably still there, right up to the time the grenade went off. Otherwise, he'd remember that O'Hara was missing for several days and that I came up to replace him. Maybe seeing me again will shake some of the cobwebs loose.'

'Do you really think so? You mean, he just doesn't want to remember about Mike O'Hara?'

'Something like that,' Charlie replied. He raised his eyebrows. 'Let's keep that last part just between us, shall we?'

'Oh, yes,' Tish agreed. 'That's . . . too terrible.'

It was not yet dawn when Neil Holmsworth stopped his car in front of Castlemont and he and Tish and Charles Clinton got out. Tish had called ahead, and the colonel had got Titus out of bed to be sure the night gatekeeper gave them no trouble. Even Winchell had been alerted, and was now hovering inside the door, awaiting them.

'Mr Morgan is still asleep,' he said. 'I was told not to waken him.'

'That's fine,' Tish said. 'Mr Clinton wanted to do that himself.' On the way, Charlie had told her what he

wanted to do, and now Tish led the way to the door of
Nicholas's suite, and then stood back to watch Charlie
go into action, her heart pounding at the thought that
she would soon see Nicholas again, and soon, very soon,
he would know the truth. If, along the way, his memory
came back, it would be an extra blessing.

Charlie Clinton stepped up to the door and began bat-
tering it loudly with his cane. In a few moments there
came a shout from inside the room.

'What in hell is going on?'

'What in hell are you doing, sacking out at this hour,
Lieutenant?' Charlie shouted back, continuing his
pounding.

'He wants to get Nicholas awake and emotionally
aroused,' Tish explained to her puzzled father.

There was the sound of heavy footsteps inside the room
and Nicholas's voice growling, 'What did you say?'

'I said open your damn door, Lieutenant,' Charlie
roared back. The door flew open, and Nicholas's
scowling face appeared. He focused his eyes on Charlie
Clinton. Charlie drew himself to attention and saluted
smartly.

'Lieutenant Morgan? Sergeant Clinton reporting, sir!'
he barked out in strong, military tones.

Nicholas looked confused. He stared first at Charlie
Clinton, then at Tish, then back at Charlie. He shook
his head, as if trying to rid himself of an insect, then
blinked rapidly. Then he leaned towards Charlie, peering
into his face.

'Say...say what you said again,' he said.

Charlie repeated, salute and all, 'Lieutenant Morgan?
Sergeant Clinton reporting, sir.' Then he added,
'O'Hara's replacement, sir.'

Nicholas stared for a few seconds more, then his mouth fell open. His eyes grew wide with disbelief.

'My God!' he cried, 'Charlie! You made it!' He threw his arms around Charlie Clinton and swept the smaller man off his feet. 'You made it! You made it!' he repeated.

Watching Nicholas, the tears of happiness streaming down his cheeks, Tish suddenly felt a great calm descending over her. Nicholas remembered. Now he would know. The calm became a lightness, her head spun. She turned towards her father and slowly fainted into his arms.

CHAPTER TWELVE

TISH awoke to a sun-filled room. Above her was an ornate ceiling, light shimmering from gilded angels in the corners, and beneath her fingers a satin coverlet.

'Good afternoon, my love,' said a deep, soft voice.

'Nicholas!' Tish turned her head, and reached out her hand towards the tall man who came toward her, his own smile so warm and beautiful that tears of happiness came to her eyes. There was a look of deep peace about his face that she had never seen before. 'Is it afternoon already?' she asked as she sat up and held out her arms to him, sighing with utter joy and contentment as he sat down beside her and gathered her close.

'It is,' he replied, his eyes scanning her face carefully. 'How do you feel?'

'Wonderful,' she said. 'I don't think I need to ask how you feel. I'm so sorry I fainted and missed the rest of your reunion with Charlie.'

Nicholas suddenly crushed her tightly against him.

'My wonderful, courageous, indomitable Tish,' he murmured in her ear. 'How can I ever thank you for what you've done for me? And how can I ever make up for all of the pain I've caused you?' He leaned back and looked into Tish's radiantly happy face. 'I guess maybe I know the answer to that,' he said.

'If you think the answer is that you don't have to,' she replied, gazing into eyes that were the clear, bright blue of a summer sky. 'Seeing you happy is all that I've ever wanted.'

Nicholas stroked her hair gently away from her face and kissed her lips very softly. 'If I have you with me for the rest of my life, I will be,' he said.

'Don't doubt for a moment that you will have,' Tish replied. She reached up and caressed his cheek. 'Can you tell me about what happened after I...left the party, so to speak?'

'In a little while,' Nicholas replied, smiling. 'Right now I just want to hold you and love you and think how very lucky I am to have you. May I ask you to marry me all over again, with no shadows in the way?'

'You may,' Tish replied, 'but it isn't necessary. I'm still wearing your ring.' She held out her hand for Nicholas to see.

Very carefully, Nicholas slid the ring from Tish's finger, then carried her hand to his lips.

'Letitia Prudence Holmsworth, will you marry me?' he asked.

'Yes, Nicholas...Nicholas, what is your middle name?' Tish asked.

'That, my love,' said Nicholas firmly, a twinkle of mischief in his eyes, 'is something you'll never know. A simple W will have to suffice.'

'Wolfgang?' Tish suggested. 'Wilberforce?'

'Tish!'

Tish giggled. 'All right, but I'm warning you: I'll find out some day. Yes, Nicholas W Morgan, I will marry you. And the sooner, the better, I might add.'

'I'll second that,' Nicholas said, slowly sliding the ring back on to Tish's finger. 'Would Sunday be soon enough? That's four days from now. I think I can arrange to cut through some red tape so we can be married then.'

'Oh, Nicholas,' Tish cried, flinging her arms around his neck, 'that would be perfect.' She frowned. 'Aren't you going to kiss me?' Nicholas's eyes were wandering over her face, resting hungrily on her lips, but he was not moving.

'I'm sitting here wondering if I dare, here on this bed,' he replied. 'I've lain here, night after night, wanting you so much, dreaming of having you here, but so afraid that if I let you come back to me it would be only a beautiful dream that would be shattered again.' He smiled ruefully and touched his lips softly to hers. 'I guess I'm having trouble adjusting to everything that's happened,' he said. 'It's not a dream, is it? It never really was.'

Tish shook her head. 'No, my darling. It never really was.'

She held her breath, watching as Nicholas's lips came closer again, her eyes holding his, then closing as his mouth covered hers, his arms tightened around her, and she was transported into a world where only the two of them existed. With boundless joy they sought ever deeper knowledge of each other, tongues searching and exploring. With delicate fingers, Tish lifted Nicholas's soft sweater and touched his skin, unsure of how well his burns had healed, not wanting to hurt him.

'It doesn't hurt,' he said, understanding. 'There are a few sensitive spots, but don't worry. Having you touch me is heaven.'

'Mmm,' Tish said, as he pushed down the shoulder-straps of the slip she still wore and caressed her bare skin, 'I know what you mean. Do we still have to wait until we're married to make love? If it's only four days...' She slid her hand inside the waistband of Nicholas's trousers and moved it across his stomach, her own desire growing as she heard him draw in his breath sharply. 'After all,' she murmured seductively, 'we've already waited a lot longer than I'd planned to.'

'I think you've just convinced me,' Nicholas said, groaning as Tish plunged her hand ever deeper. He tumbled her back against the pillows and then flung the coverlet aside. 'Do your worst to me, woman,' he said, pulling off his sweater and then lying down beside her. 'Take your time. If the phone rings this time, I'll throw it out of the window.'

Carefully, Tish removed Nicholas's remaining clothing, stroking him with loving hands that made him sigh with pleasure. In minutes he had done the same for her, feathering kisses over each new inch of her bare skin that he uncovered until she was dizzy from the electrifying sensations that soared through her body. They moved their naked bodies together, touching each other, holding each other close, but very still. To Tish it felt as if they had already become one, their hearts beating together, their breath falling warm and soft on each other's lips.

'I love you, Nicholas,' she murmured, stroking his silken hair.

'I love you, Tish,' he replied. His mouth sought hers again, his hands began to move, caressing, gently teasing. He cupped her breasts and then eagerly sought their rosy peaks with his lips.

Tish caught her breath, overwhelmed by the sudden rush of ecstasy his movements sent coursing through her. When he followed the path of longing he had created, she heard herself making soft little noises of pleasure, as if soaring in a world where sensation and sound were one. When it seemed she must surely plunge from the giddy heights, she raised her head, her eyes beseeching, her arms outstretched. Nicholas smiled and answered, rising above her and at last making her his alone on a journey that sent Tish flying to the stars, and then returning through wondrous clouds of dreamy hues, changing from glowing rose to soft peach, and then to the blue of Nicholas's eyes, watching her and smiling.

'I think I've just been to heaven and back,' she murmured, caressing his cheek. 'Is it always like that?'

'I think for us it will be,' he answered, cradling her in the curve of his shoulder. He watched Tish's face as she traced the outline of his scars with her finger. 'I can have those taken off now,' he said. 'The doctors say they can pretty well make them disappear.'

Tish looked into his eyes, and then back at the scars. 'Don't do it for me,' she said. 'I love you just the way you are—but if it will make you happy, do it.'

'I'll think about it for a while,' Nicholas said. 'I think you deserve a better-looking husband, but I've seen enough of hospitals to last me for some time.' He sighed. 'I suppose we should get dressed. Charlie and your father are still here. I don't want Charlie to leave without my having a chance to thank him again, and I want to see if he can come back and be my best man. With that plane of his, he ought to be able to.'

'That's a wonderful idea,' Tish replied. 'But you still haven't told me one thing about what happened this morning after I fainted. I wish I hadn't. I did so want to hear what you'd say.'

'I think the first thing I said was, "Good lord, what's wrong with Tish?"' Nicholas said with a chuckle, sitting up and beginning to put his clothes on. 'Then I dropped poor Charlie like a hot potato, picked you up, and carried you in here. The consensus was that you were exhausted, so we let you sleep, but I kept looking in every couple of minutes to make sure you were all right.'

'Did you remember everything right away?' Tish asked. 'Or was it like a movie, coming a little at a time?'

'You know,' Nicholas said thoughtfully, 'I'm not really sure. When I recognised Charlie, it was as if everything fell into place at once. I didn't have to review what happened. It was just there. I remembered what Mike had done, how angry I was about it, but it didn't hit me like a brick. Even now, when I think about it, it's more like a feeling of tremendous disappointment.'

'But he tried to kill you!' Tish cried.

Nicholas shook his head. 'You mean the grenade? I'm not sure he knew what he was doing. He'd been into something he shouldn't have. Anyway,' he shrugged, 'that's all water over the dam now. I can't live with past regrets. I have you and our future to think about now.' He turned his head and smiled as Tish, now dressed in her slip, stood up and put her hand on his arm.

'Nicholas,' she said seriously, 'that's very noble of you, but aren't you even going to tell him that you remember now and know he lied to you? Think of the years of misery he caused you!'

'I don't think so,' Nicholas replied. 'Charlie and your dad and I talked about that. They thought I'd be bitter, and in a way I am. But there's no point in it. I just want to get on with my... with *our* life now. I'll let Mike find out from someone else, as he doubtless will. Then he can spend the rest of his life wondering why I haven't.'

Tish put her arms around Nicholas's waist and hugged him, leaning her cheek against his chest. 'I think you're absolutely right about not looking back. I know you are. It makes me terribly angry, but I'll do my best not to let it bother me, either. There's one other thing, though...'

'What's that, my love?' Nicholas asked, tilting her chin up with his hand. 'If it's more about old Mike, I'd just soon forget it, now that I remember. I have more pleasant things to think about now.' He bent his head and kissed the tip of her nose.

'Just this one,' Tish said. After hearing Charlie's horrid tale of Mike O'Hara's jealousy, she wondered if Nicholas had any idea that that was why he had lied. She smiled up at her tall, handsome man. 'I should think,' she said, 'that you'd be curious about why Mike lied to you in the first place, if he was supposed to be your friend. You don't seem to think that he truly meant to kill you with that grenade.'

'Why Mike lied?' Nicholas sighed. 'I think I know. Charlie Clinton helped me understand what his motivation could have been. Love and hate can be very close together, you know. I think that when Mike thought he'd killed me, he was a little bit glad, deep inside. I knew Mike was always terribly jealous of me. He thought I didn't know it, but I did. Probably the more he thought about it, the more easily he was able to get over the guilt he felt by thinking about the fact that I wasn't around to compete against any more. Then, when I reappeared and couldn't remember, he thought of the perfect way to get me out of the picture again. He knew how strongly I was devoted to my men, and what it would do to me if I thought I had failed them. I guess I'll never know what really went wrong that day now, but at least I know it wasn't my fault, although...' he sighed heavily, 'I'll never get over the feeling of loss.'

Tish put her hands on his shoulders. 'You, Lieutenant Morgan,' she said, 'are a remarkable, wonderful man.'

And Charlie Clinton was a remarkable man, too, she thought. He had helped Nicholas to understand what had happened, without actually telling him the terrible details. She smiled brightly. 'All right, remarkable, wonderful man, now that the subject is closed, do you happen to remember where you put my dress and shoes?'

'Yes, ma'am,' Nicholas replied, his own smile returning quickly. He went to the armoire and retrieved them. 'I must admit, I rather enjoyed removing that dress from you when I put you to bed,' he teased. 'You kept mumbling and making the cutest little noises.'

'I wish I could remember,' Tish said, making a face at him as she slipped into her dress, and then turned her back to Nicholas. 'You may as well learn right now, husband-to-be, that one of the reasons women marry is to have someone to zip them up.'

'Looks like fun to me,' Nicholas said, quickly doing his duty. He turned Tish around, and then suddenly crushed her against him. 'Oh, my darling,' he murmured, 'I'm so happy now. I'd go through it all again if I had to in order to be where I am right now, with you.'

Tish blinked back the tears of happiness that sprang to her eyes. 'I'm darned if I'd let you,' she said, sniffing slightly. 'There's got to be an easier way.'

Nicholas chuckled. 'It does seem that way, doesn't it? Well, shall we go and give everyone the good news?'

'Let's do,' Tish agreed. 'And if I call Mavis and Mrs Braman, everyone in Laketown will know about the wedding by sundown.'

'Then, by all means call them,' Nicholas said, grinning. 'Hire a town crier, if you want to. But warn everyone that on such short notice, it's going to be a small affair. Only the Greers, and all the people at the *Herald* who worked so hard to help you find Charlie.'

'Peggy Willson's the one who did,' Tish said. 'I'd have her be my maid of honour, except that would make Mavis mad. I wonder if I could have two?'

'I don't see why not,' Nicholas said. 'After all we've been through, we deserve to make our own rules.'

Tish proved right about the town being abuzz with news of their wedding by sundown. Early that evening the phone at Tish's house, where she and Nicholas and her father were relaxing after the excitement of the day, began ringing. In the end, there were so many people who really should be invited that the little church on the square in Laketown was packed to overflowing on Sunday afternoon, and banked with so many flowers that Tish was sure there was not a florist for miles around who had a single blossom left.

Tish had argued that she had no time for elaborate preparations, but Mrs Greer, Mavis's mother, had stepped into the breach, enlisting friends and neighbours to prepare the church for the ceremony and the grand salon at Castlemont for the reception. She laboured frantically herself, providing Tish with a lovely traditional gown trimmed in seed-pearls and lace, with an heirloom veil from her own family.

'Break it in for Mavis,' the kindly woman said, giving her own daughter a meaningful look. 'Just be sure she catches your bouquet.'

As Tish walked down the aisle on her father's arm, she was sure there was no woman in the world as happy as she. Nicholas watched her approaching, his smile enveloping her in loving warmth, his arm reaching out to draw her close to him so that he could whisper that he loved her once again before the ceremony began. When, at last, the minister announced that Nicholas might kiss his bride, Tish melted into Nicholas's arms, wanting that precious moment to last for ever. It was only when she heard a murmur in the assembled crowd that she realised it was time for them to leave the church, now husband and wife.

The reception at Castlemont was lovely, but Tish soon sensed that her husband was tiring of the company. As soon as they had done their duty, receiving the guests and cutting the wedding cake, she drew him aside.

'Am I mistaken, dear husband, or is there something you'd rather be doing?' she asked, casting him a coquettish glance.

'Mrs Morgan, I do believe you're clairvoyant,' Nicholas replied. 'But, given that we're staying here, how do we get out of this mess? Sneak up the back stairs?'

'An excellent idea,' Tish said. 'I doubt if anyone will miss us.'

Nicholas smiled, a devilish gleam in his eyes. 'My dear,' he said, taking her hand and leading her toward the door, 'I don't give a damn whether they do or not.'

EPILOGUE

IT WAS only a week after the wedding that Lady Whirlwind's foal, a miniature Titan, was born. To Tish's surprise, Nicholas was only quietly happy at the event.

'I should think you'd be turning handsprings,' she told him.

Nicholas smiled. 'Horses aren't everything in the world to me any more,' he said. 'If you want to see excitement, just wait until we have a child.' He looked towards the new stables that were under construction. 'I'll teach all the children to be excellent riders, but it will be strictly for recreation. Not an obsession.'

It was only a few weeks later that Tish announced to Nicholas that their first child was on the way. Just the expectation made Nicholas exuberantly happy, distributing chocolate cigars around Laketown as if the event had already occurred.

'What on earth are you going to do for an encore when the baby comes?' Tish demanded.

'How about a fireworks display?' Nicholas replied, laughing. 'Or, since it will be at Christmas time, I could put on a Santa Claus suit and hand out presents to everyone in Laketown.'

'I don't think you're fat enough to be jolly old Saint Nicholas,' Tish teased, 'or quite saintly enough, either.' She managed to squelch some of his wilder ideas before the baby arrived, but he did sponsor a huge Christmas party for all of the Laketown children, and proudly gave the whole town free copies of the *Laketown Herald*, with a picture of Tish, holding young Charles Clinton Morgan in her arms, on the front page.

It was spring again when Winchell came into the library at Castlemont, where Tish and Nicholas and baby Charlie were enjoying a leisurely breakfast together.

'A Mr Mike O'Hara to see you, sir,' he announced to Nicholas.

Tish gasped. Nicholas gave her a quick, surprised look and then followed Winchell back into the foyer. Tish, holding the baby in her arms, followed.

Mike O'Hara stood quietly, pale and thin and seeming very small in the huge expanse of the foyer. His face was lined and anxious-looking. He seemed unable to look at Nicholas for more than a moment, then stared down at the floor. Nicholas stopped in front of him, and Tish saw that her husband's expression was more curious than cold or angry.

'What did you want, Mike?' he asked quietly.

Mike glanced up, then away again. 'I came to see if I could borrow some of your courage,' he said softly. 'I've been wondering lately if it's worth going on with my life.'

'Good lord, man!' Nicholas said, immediately concerned. 'Don't even think of such a thing!' He put his arm around Mike's shoulders. 'Come in and talk a while.'

For over an hour, Tish listened quietly while the two men talked. At last, Mike O'Hara left.

'Do you think he'll be all right?' Tish asked, seeing the worried lines around her husband's eyes.

'I don't know.' Nicholas looked down at Tish and smiled, then took Charlie from her and held him close, his face against the baby's warm, downy head. 'I don't think there's anything I can do to give Mike the peace he's looking for,' he said. 'The kind that I have found.'

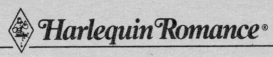
Harlequin Romance®

Coming Next Month

2995 SOME ENCHANTED EVENING Jenny Arden
Eve has to admit that Zack Thole is persistent, and wickedly
handsome, but she is almost committed to Greg and has no
intention of being carried away by moonlight and madness. Yet
Zack can be very persuasive....

2996 LORD OF THE LODGE Miriam MacGregor
Lana comes to New Zealand's Kapiti coast to find the father she's
never known, having discovered he works at the Leisure Lodge
guest house. Owner Brent Tremaine, however, completely
misinterprets her interest in his employee. Surely he can't
be jealous?

2997 SHADES OF YESTERDAY Leigh Michaels
Necessity forces Courtney to approach old Nate Winslow for help.
After all, Nate owes her something—her mother had said so—
though Courtney doesn't know what. So it annoys her that his son
Jeff regards her as an undesirable scrounger!

2998 LOVE ON A STRING Celia Scott
Bryony not only designs and makes kites, she loves flying them—
and Knucklerock Field is just the right spot. When Hunter Green
declares his intention to turn it into a helicopter base, it's like a
declaration of war between them!

2999 THE HUNGRY HEART Margaret Way
Liane has steered clear of Julian Wilde since their divorce. But when
Jonathon, her small stepson, needs her help, she just can't stay
away—even though it means facing Julian again. After all, it isn't as
if he still loved her.

3000 THE LOST MOON FLOWER
Bethany Campbell

"Whitewater, I want you." These three desperate words not only
move lone hunter Aaron Whitewater to guide Josie through the
treacherous mountains of a tiny Hawaiian island to retrieve a
priceless stolen panda, they prove dangerously prophetic....

Available in August wherever paperback books are sold, or
through Harlequin Reader Service:

In the U.S.
901 Fuhrmann Blvd.
P.O. Box 1397
Buffalo, N.Y. 14240-1397

In Canada
P.O. Box 603
Fort Erie, Ontario
L2A 5X3

ANNOUNCING . . .

The Lost Moon Flower
by Bethany Campbell

Look for it this August
wherever Harlequins are sold

HR 3000-1

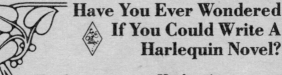

Have You Ever Wondered If You Could Write A Harlequin Novel?

Here's great news—Harlequin is offering a series of cassette tapes to help you do just that. Written by Harlequin editors, these tapes give practical advice on how to make your characters—and your story—come alive. There's a tape for each contemporary romance series Harlequin publishes.

Mail order only

All sales final

TO: **_Harlequin Reader Service_**
Audiocassette Tape Offer
P.O. Box 1396
Buffalo, NY 14269-1396

I enclose a check/money order payable to HARLEQUIN READER SERVICE® for $9.70 ($8.95 plus 75¢ postage and handling) for EACH tape ordered for the total sum of $_____*
Please send:

☐ Romance and Presents   ☐ Intrigue
☐ American Romance   ☐ Temptation
☐ Superromance   ☐ All five tapes ($38.80 total)

Signature_____
                                    (please print clearly)
Name:_____

Address:_____

State:_____ Zip:_____

*Iowa and New York residents add appropriate sales tax.   AUDIO-H

Harlequin American Romance.

The sun, the surf, the sand...

One relaxing month by the sea was all Zoe,
Diana and Gracie ever expected from their
four-week stay at Gull Cottage, the luxurious
East Hampton mansion. They never thought
that what they found at the beach would
change their lives forever.

Join Zoe, Diana and Gracie for the summer of
their lives. Don't miss the GULL COTTAGE
trilogy in Harlequin American Romance: #301
CHARMED CIRCLE by Robin Francis (July
1989); #305 MOTHER KNOWS BEST by
Barbara Bretton (August 1989); and #309
SAVING GRACE by Anne McAllister
(September 1989).

GULL COTTAGE—because one month can be
the start of forever...

Harlequin American Romance

**Romances that go one step farther...
American Romance**

Realistic stories involving people you can relate to and
care about.

Compelling relationships between the mature men and
women of today's world.

Romances that capture the core of genuine emotions
between a man and a woman.

Join us each month for four new titles wherever paperback
books are sold.
Enter the world of American Romance.

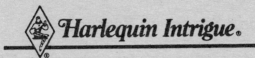 *Harlequin Intrigue*®

They went in through the terrace door. The house was dark, most of the servants were down at the circus, and only Nelbert's hired security guards were in sight. It was child's play for Blackheart to move past them, the work of two seconds to go through the solid lock on the terrace door. And then they were creeping through the darkened house, up the long curving stairs, Ferris fully as noiseless as the more experienced Blackheart.

They stopped on the second floor landing. "What if they have guns?" Ferris mouthed silently.

Blackheart shrugged. "Then duck."

"How reassuring," she responded. Footsteps directly above them signaled that the thieves were on the move, and so should they be.

For more romance, suspense and adventure, read Harlequin Intrigue. Two exciting titles each month, available wherever Harlequin Books are sold.